PROMISE ME FOREVER

BINDARRA CREEK – A TOWN REBORN

JUANITA KEES

CONTENTS

EXCERPT - HOME TO BINDARRA CREEK

PROMISE ME FOREVER

Bindarra Creek
A Town Reborn

JUANITA KEES

Published by Juanita Kees (Kees2Create)

Paperback 978-0-6484995-3-4

eBook 978-0-6484995-4-1

Large Print 978-0-6484995-5-8

Cover Design © By Paradox Book Cover & Formatting

Edited by Teena Raffa

ACKNOWLEDGEMENTS

Thank you to S E (Suzanne) Gilchrist and the Bindarra Creek authors who have made our town so real we all want to live there. We have created a warm, wonderful Australian rural community and have captured the true spirit of our beautiful country. I am proud to be a part of this group venture and value the long-lasting friendships forged over the years.

Thank you to S E (Suzanne) Gilchrist for allowing me to use the history of Bindarra Creek in this story. All copyright for the existence of the town and its history belong to S E Gilchrist.

To my critique group and mentors – Anna Jacobs, Claire Boston, Susanna Rogers, Teena Raffa-Mulligan and Lorraine Mauvais – your input is always valuable. My writing has grown in strength with your support and guidance.

A special thanks to Teena who took on the task of editing my work with her years of expertise. To the fabulous Lily Malone, you're my rock throughout the dirty draft and a valued friend. Thank you for sharing my writing journey.

And of course, to my family. Thank you to Gav and the boys for feeding and watering me, and for supplying the chocolate, wine and endless cups of tea when I'm on deadline.

Thank you, Mum, for buying and reading my books and being my biggest fan. And, Dad, thank you for sharing your talent for storytelling with me.

DEDICATION

To the readers of Australian Rural Romance Fiction,
thank you.
You have made these stories possible.

© S E Gilchrist (Used with permission from the author)

Bindarra Creek was founded in 1842 initially as little more than a staging depot for supplies to the new settlers in the area who began to arrive in 1839 and also as a change of horses / bullock teams / stay over for people travelling from Armidale to Moree.

Prior to this, the area was originally the site of several large grazing properties and was populated with a mix of free settlers and convict servants.

There were two working gold mines nearby which brought an influx of both people and money into the town and it grew steadily.

By 1850 the township had started to grow with a catholic church (more like a one room hovel) and school being built. There was a small store which carried basic needs other than what people grew and three public houses. Often bartering went on between the town people to help each other out.

The town was in full swing by 1858.

The Church of England, St Ignatius was built in 1861 and was a wattle and daub hut. The current church was built in 1882 from locally sourced bricks on the site of the original church.

During the 1860's the famous bushranger roamed the area, Captain Thunderbolt, robbing properties of horses, mail coaches and inns.

One of the public houses (inn/pub) was burnt to the ground in 1902.

In 1985 a massive flood caused considerable damage to the town and some deaths (including Pamela Brown's husband and 18-year-old son, both are buried in the BC cemetery).

Descendants of the first settlers to the area remain in Bindarra Creek at present time. At the time the first series Bindarra Creek Romance was set, the population had dwindled to 2079 and the gold mines were depleted.

Thanks to a government grant (2015), the Bindarra Creek Progress Association and the determination of the ladies of the CWA, the town is growing in economy, size and population.

The first Bindarra Creek Arts and Crafts festival was held in September 2018 and included the first Scavenger Challenge. The festival was a great success, bringing more publicity and consequently fresh blood to town.

(Note: the bones of Bindarra Creek's history were modelled on the early history of Manilla NSW)

CHAPTER ONE

*J*ack Hughes hitched his backpack higher onto his shoulder, perched his sunglasses on his head, loosened another button on his shirt and contemplated all the things he'd done wrong in his life to deserve being sent to hell.

Bindarra Creek, somewhere between Armidale and Moree, a town reborn out of fire and flood and God only knew what else. A dot on the map of New South Wales where a few die-hards hung onto hope that new life could be breathed into the quiet streets.

A town where his producer had sent Jack to lick his wounds. Out of the spotlight, away from trolling Twitter feeds, heartless critics and fake news click bait.

And to make matters worse, he'd had to walk the last four kilometres because his beloved EH Holden, Betty, had carked it on the outskirts of town with steam pouring from under her bonnet. Now she was at the mercy of any passing road trains that would likely sweep her right off the side of the road in their side draft.

As if poor Betty hadn't suffered enough after his ex-girlfriend had taken a knife to her right-hand side fender and left her scarred for life. An action sparked by a whole string of unfortunate events he didn't want to think about when his feet were on fire in his shoes.

Reaching the street address his boss had given him, Jack waved off the flies and opened the rusted chain link garden gate outside Mary Moonie's Museum. As he stepped onto the cracked concrete path, the tune from *Deliverance* played on a loop between his ears. The place was a verandah post short of falling in a heap.

The old iron roof sagged, red paint making way for a coat of brown rust. Dust coated the glass of the wood-framed windows, the paint chipped and peeling. All it needed was a bloke on the verandah with a shotgun, and his producer's day would be made.

With a grimace and a prayer that the warped door marked 'entry' wouldn't fall off its rusty hinges, Jack pushed it open. He blinked against the brightness of the fluorescent lighting inside what once might have been an impressive gift shop and entry display. Relics from the town's tumultuous history now looked worse for wear and bore a few obvious signs of water damage.

Jack welcomed the blast of cool air that touched his face. At least the air conditioning was fairly modern.

He eyed the rumbling unit — probably fitted in the seventies — with dubious delight. The door squealed shut behind him. Dabbing at the sweat on his forehead with his bandanna, he approached the 1920s counter and the lady behind it.

Only about twenty-odd years younger than the shop counter, she looked ready for a day at the races. Black fringed dress dating back to the era of swing bands and jazz clubs, clip-on earrings he remembered seeing in old photos from the fifties and sixties, and a fascinator in her recently coloured, rusty-blonde hair. A multitude of mixed vintage bangles circled her left wrist while her right one sported a dainty marcasite watch. She would have been one classy lady back in her day.

"G'day," he said.

She smiled at him, tipping her reading glasses lower on her nose. "G'day, love. What can I help you with today? We have our self-guided tour on special at thirty dollars."

Self-guided tour of what? The crumbling dunny out the back? Jack flashed his press pass and returned her smile, his mouth dry and his lips a little sunburned. "Jack Hughes from Channel Eight, *Outback Affairs*." The words soured on his tongue. He used to be Jack Hughes, *International News*. His producer hadn't even lined up the film crew yet, not sure there was even a story worth covering out here in The Arse End of Nowhere. "Here to cover the story of Mary Moonie and Bindarra Creek, a town reborn."

He tried to keep cynicism from colouring his tone and failed. He'd done his research. Reluctantly. How many chances did a town get at rebirth before the residents gave up?

"That'll be forty-five dollars entry fee then." The smile froze on her lips and she pushed her glasses firmly onto the bridge of her nose.

"Forty— What? Are you serious?" All Jack wanted was a cold drink from the antique fridge, but now he was too scared to ask the price.

"Does this look like the kind of face that would crack a joke? This isn't just any old museum, you know. This is where Mary Moonie lived. And where she died. Right there in that corner." She pointed at the rocking chair in the corner of the shop, her black-painted pointy nails almost claw-like on her crooked, arthritic fingers. "Her life has historical significance. Don't mess with me or I'll up it to sixty dollars." She rang up the threatened amount on a cash register straight out of an old western movie and held out her hand. "And for the record, I didn't want the press involved. Cash only, no credit."

"Aunty Phyllis!"

Jack turned toward the back of the shop and Hell suddenly got a lot more interesting as an angel dropped in. Or maybe he had heatstroke. A woman with white-blonde hair and almost translucent skin, wearing khaki shorts, a hot pink T-shirt, steel-capped boots and a breath-stealing smile emerged from the shadows at the rear of the shop.

"You must be Jack?"

Soft, silvery tones tickled his spine, fizzed his blood and tied his tongue in knots. He nodded as she approached. In the flicker of the fluorescent light above the counter, her skin glowed soft and pearly, like the satin of his sheets at home. Her eyes met his, neither green nor blue but some captivating colour in between. His breath hitched in his throat.

"This is my Aunty Phyllis and I'm Meg, Mary's granddaughter."

Jack couldn't help but stare at her exquisite features as he engulfed her delicate hand in his. A flash of fire spread in his belly at the sparkle in her eyes. Hooley dooley hotness. He remembered a story one of his teachers had told at school once about a fairy who lived in the outback and lured men into the bush with her beauty. For the first time since his childhood, Jack wondered if the legend was true, because the girl with her hand in his was truly something else.

His brain ramped back into gear as the raspy cackle of the extortionist behind the counter broke the spell that bound his tongue.

"Jack Hughes, *Outback Affairs*. I believe my producer contacted you?" Reluctantly, he let her hand go when she tugged at it, and the blood fizzed back into his head along with what was left of his common sense.

Women were trouble and he couldn't let this one distract him from his job or he'd never get back to reality.

"Yes, we were expecting you to arrive hours ago. Come with me and I'll take you over to the Riverside Pub. That's where you'll be staying while you're in town." She shook a warning finger at the old dear behind the counter. "Aunty Phyl, stop trying to rip off the tourists. We want to encourage them to come inside, not chase them away," she said as she swept past Jack, opened the fridge, and took out a bottle of water.

"Got to get cash flowing into this mausoleum somehow, my girl."

"Not that way. And it's a *museum*, thank you very much. If Granny Mary heard you call it a mausoleum, she'd come back to haunt you." Meg handed Jack the bottle of water. "Here you go. It's hot out there today. I'm sure you'd kill for a beer instead."

Aunty Phyllis huffed out a breath. "I'd use those words lightly considering what happened to Mary."

"There's no proof she was poisoned." Meg shot a warning look across the counter then turned to Jack to explain, "Her heart gave out."

See, no story at all. Jack shifted on his feet, thinking that, in this possibly crazy town, he'd still sniff whatever was handed to him anyway, just in case. Could you smell poison?

"Right." Aunty Phyllis drew the word out on a sceptical note. "You tell that to those fancy city laboratory people next time they're testing the drinking water. Someone is trying to kill the people in this town."

Meg shook her head. "The contamination could have happened after the flood. All kinds of chemicals and junk got washed into the river when it rose. Come along, Jack. The beer is bottled in Sydney and the drinking water has been given the all clear. As long as you don't go consuming still water from any billabongs out in the bush, you're okay. Besides, Dan who owns the Riverside Pub wouldn't kill a fly."

"Or a cockroach," muttered Phyllis with a pointed look at Jack as she reached for the fly spray beside her. "Gotta keep the pests under control, you know."

With a quick look at Aunty Phyllis, Jack dropped his sunnies over his eyes and followed Meg out the door onto the pavement. What the hell kind of town had his boss sent him to?

The view on the other hand was pretty damn pleasing. Meg had a sway to her hips that was easy to watch. A man could get used to that. If he was in the market. But with Kelsey leaving him over the stir Tamryn Hollister had caused with that fake video, he'd be avoiding women for a while.

Shit! How could he have forgotten all about Betty? Jack dragged his gaze from Meg's hips. "Wait! My car. I had to leave it down the road. She overheated. Any chance we could get it towed in?" He stopped and waited for her to turn around.

"Oh no. That could be a problem. Is it a rental?"

"No, she's all mine." He couldn't help the proud grin that split his face because even beat up, Betty was the love of his life. The only girl who hadn't given him any trouble. Until today.

"Oh dear."

He didn't like the tightening of her lips or the frown that brought her perfect eyebrows closer together. "What do you mean 'oh dear'?"

"Ever since Nobby Wilkie went bush after Mary died, some of the local kids have been collecting abandoned cars to build a spirit garden to bring him back. Nobby likes to tinker and he teaches the kids how to fix things."

A headache began a slow thump behind Jack's eyes. He pushed his sunglasses back up onto his head and rubbed the bridge of his nose. He couldn't let Betty die abandoned on the side of the road. She was all he had left.

Meg's warm, comforting touch on his arm had him dropping his hand from his face to look into those fairy eyes once more. Maybe she had a magic wand or something she could wave.

"Betty's a classic," he said, as if that would explain everything.

"Ahh..." She dragged the sound out on a sigh that sent pleasant shivers down his spine. "I get it. How about this? I'll drag *my* old ute out of the garage and we'll go and collect Betty. We'll have to work fast though, so that beer I promised you might have to wait."

"What do you mean 'work fast'?" He needed to get a handle on his words so he didn't keep repeating hers like a moron.

She stepped from foot to foot, squirming a little. "It's just ... well ... she could be mistaken for a wreck depending on the condition she's in and, if that's the case, you might find she's missing a few parts when we get there."

Jack cursed his boss, his ex-girlfriend, the bloody viral click bait video, *and* the town of Bindarra Creek as the vision of Betty — stripped bare — swam in his vision. God, he hated shitty backwater towns.

"Don't worry, Jack. Betty will be just fine. The kids will still be in school." Meg glanced at the watch on her wrist, rubbing at a splash of varnish on the skin above it. "Or at least, they should be." Lord, she hoped so. Should she throw a couple of spare wheel rims and tyres into the back of the ute just in case? "Follow me."

She led the way through the museum gate, down the pathway, past the white park bench where Granny Mary and Edwina Lette used to sit and drink tea and opened the gates on the driveway to the house next door.

Poor Jack. He must think he'd strayed onto the set

of a prank show after meeting Aunty Phyllis. She chuckled. Wait until Friday night karaoke at the Riverside Pub. He'd be in for a treat then.

Jack. Cute in a guy-next-door kind of a way with his city-styled hair and a day or two's growth of dark beard lining his jaw. But he was a reporter just like the slippery, snake-tongued pretty boy Logan had been. Logan who'd come to town on an assignment and broken her heart with his sweet promises and zero delivery.

Then his wife had turned up with their gorgeous baby girl for a visit from Armidale to surprise him. She'd surprised Meg and everyone else in town who'd thought he was single. He'd left with his family that same day, narrowly avoiding a CWA-organised lynch mob. *Don't let the door hit you on the arse on your way out of town, Logan McGee.*

Granny Mary had made her a cup of tea because tea fixed everything. Nobby had held out his handkerchief to dry her tears. Aunty Phyllis had offered her a glass of champagne and a cigar to celebrate.

How things had changed in a year. Sadness squeezed at her chest. Granny Mary had been gone six weeks and — heartbroken by her death — Nobby was still walkabout after three. Hope for him coming back under his own steam was fading fast in Meg's heart. Ranger Alice had scoured the bush of the Akuna

National Park for him and found no clues as to his whereabouts.

But Nobby was a man used to disappearing like a spirit of the night. A long walk in the outback could mean weeks or months and any direction on the compass. An experienced trail-walker, he'd gone bush before for long periods of time and he'd always come back. She had to hang onto hope.

"Meg?"

The query in Jack's tone brought her back to the present. She bent down and wrapped her hand around the handle of the old garage door, hefted it up and let the weights do their job to open it all the way. Granny Mary's old yellow ute stood nose-out in the shadows, the rusty old grille greeting her like the smile of an old friend.

Behind her, Jack barked out a laugh, loud in the silence. "You're going to tow me with that? Give it another few years and you could put it in your museum."

"Now, Jack, don't be like that. This ute is unbreakable. We've tested its strength many times over the years."

He came to stand beside her, hands on his hips, his sunglasses perched on his head, smelling like sunshine and something citrusy. "Yeah? I have my doubts."

"Well, hop in and I'll dispel them for you." Meg opened the driver's door and climbed in. Jack climbed in beside her.

"Don't you need a key?" He yanked at the seatbelt a few times until it released then hooked it into the clip.

Smiling, she searched under the dash with her hands and located the green and red wires. She touched them together and the engine started. Then she taped them up with a piece of electrical tape stuck to the dashboard. "This is the country, city boy. We make do. I don't even know where the keys are. I don't remember ever seeing them. Granny Mary most likely lost them somewhere the day she drove it out of the dealership back in the eighties."

Pulling on her own seatbelt, Meg eased the ute out onto the driveway. "How far out of town did you leave the car?"

Jack shrugged. "About four kilometres."

"You walked all that way?" Quite a hike in fancy leather shoes made for office parties and lounging around in cocktail bars.

"I've walked further. In the right shoes," he mumbled.

"You'll have blisters the size of eggs in those." Meg upped the ute's speed to the limit as they passed the showground paddocks. "I can ask our local psychic and healer, Edwina, if she has some tissue salts to soak your feet in?"

"What? No! Thank you, I'm sure my feet will survive."

She wanted to tease the horrified frown from his

brow. Clearly, Jack Hughes was way out of his depth in his city shoes. "Relax, Jack. I'm pulling your leg. About the shoes. Not about Edwina, though. I'm guessing you're not a fan of the country?"

He shrugged. "I wouldn't say that. I've done my fair share of hiking around strange places on assignments. I prefer the excitement of the city, that's all."

Meg stifled a laugh. "Yes, Aunty Phyllis has been following the excitement of your ... adventures ... quite closely."

Jack groaned and dropped his head back against the worn headrest. "Really?"

This time the laugh escaped. "We do have television and internet out here, you know. It's sketchy at times, but we do get it. Aunty Phyllis decided it was her duty to check you out before you arrived in town. So ... a politician's daughter, huh? How did that work out for you?"

"The online video was photoshopped click bait. It didn't happen," he snapped.

"Hmm ... okay. Well, save your story of how it didn't happen for later. Is that Betty over there?" She slowed right down and pointed out the window straight ahead.

Jack lifted his head to look. "Yeah. Wait ... what are they doing?"

A group of kids circled the powder blue EH Holden where it had come to rest in the shade of the gum trees. They inspected the wheels, the paintwork, the bonnet, then congregated at the rear, nodding.

"That's the Lawson kids. Their fence runs the length of the field where you've broken down. Looks like they beat us to it. Hold onto your seatbelt, we're going to make a U-turn."

Meg executed the turn and pulled up in front of Jack's car then reversed back a little. The kids waved and ran up to them, excitement lighting up their faces as they crowded the ute.

"Jesus," muttered Jack, reaching for the door handle.

"It's okay, they don't bite. Usually." Meg laughed and opened her door to get out. "Hey, kids."

"Meg! This is it! The spirits brought it right to our door. This is the car that will bring Nobby home." Scotty, the eldest boy, hopped from one foot to the other.

The others all fell into a chorus of shouts and high-fives as the youngest girl, Indie, wrapped her arms around Meg's waist and held on tight. Meg hitched Indie up onto her hip and the girl transferred her grip to Meg's neck.

"Hang on a minute, guys. This is Jack and the car belongs to him. You can't take this one, sorry."

A chorus of 'aww' echoed around them. "But, Meg, we've got to find the right one. Time's running out."

She ran a hand over Scotty's dark curls. "I know, mate, but Jack needs his car. We'll find another one.

Aunty Phyllis has been ringing all the wreckers' yards for you."

"It's not the same." Scotty folded his arms, pouted his lips and glowered. "It has to be abandoned for the spirits to draw Nobby's attention to it."

Jack hovered protectively over Betty's damaged fender. "Well, this one is not abandoned."

"There are many abandoned cars that end up at the wreckers." She pulled the boy into a hug, which he accepted reluctantly. "Don't worry, we'll find the right one. But Jack needs his car. It's very special to him."

"Can't be that special if someone used a screwdriver on the paintwork," muttered Scotty, nodding his head toward the car.

Meg released him from the hug, hitched Indie higher and walked over to take a look. "Oh dear." She read the words carved into the otherwise flawless paintwork. "Well, that's very ... specific. The politician's daughter?"

Jack shook his head. "The ex-girlfriend."

"Mmm ... right."

Had she got herself stuck in a time warp? Because it sounded like Jack Hughes had a lot in common with Logan when it came to women. Click bait or not, his alleged wild affair had damaged his relationship enough for his ex to tell him where to go *and* carve it into the fender on his car so he didn't forget.

"Well, kids, don't go repeating those words, okay?" She put Indie down on the ground with a kiss to the little girl's cheek. "We're going to tow Jack's car back into town to get it fixed at Nobby's garage. Why don't you all go home and do your homework. Nobby would like that, I'm sure. And don't forget to give your mum a hand in the veggie garden this afternoon. It's market day on Saturday."

"Okay, Meg." They climbed the wooden access ladder that straddled the fence and took off across the field toward home, waving. Except Scotty, who strolled behind, kicking at stones and grass.

"What did they mean about the car having to be abandoned?" Jack watched as the kids disappeared from view.

Meg smiled. "Nobby rescues things. Plants, animals, people, but mostly cars. Then he fixes them up. The kids think that if they build a collection of abandoned cars and parts in their spiritual garden, the spirits will lure Nobby back from his walk in the bush."

"What else is in this spiritual garden? Aside from cars and parts." Genuine curiosity coloured his question.

"A couple of rabbits in a hutch, some dead plants, a few live ones struggling to survive, some other bits and pieces. Muttley and Curly drop in from time to time."

Frowning, Jack looked at her. "Muttley and Curly?"

"Muttley is a kangaroo Ranger Alice rescued. Her husband, Dan, raised him after he accidentally ran over Muttley's mother with his car. Curly is Old Man Jake's cockatoo. Old Man Jake — we call him that so he doesn't get confused with the much younger Jake Morgan over at Tulachmhor — is the caretaker at the Riverside Pub. Watch out for him. He's not a fan of strangers and he has a gun."

"A *gun*?"

Poor Jack. He looked like he could do with a dose of Edwina's special relaxation herbs. "Don't worry. It shoots foam pellets."

"You're having me on again, aren't you?" Now he sounded plain hopeful.

Meg grinned. "We make our own fun out here. That's why I love this town so much, Jack. There's never a dull day in Bindarra Creek. We've had fire and flood. There's been disease and destruction. We've even had run-ins with stock rustlers." She pinched her forefinger and thumb close together. "We've come *this* close to being a ghost town. But no matter what the universe throws at us, the people get back up and start over. Rebuild, regenerate, and keep fighting to save our town and its heritage."

"You're pretty passionate about it." He sounded so surprised that she laughed.

"The town, the people ... they're my life. I wouldn't trade that for anything." Meg grinned broadly up at him. "Granny Mary worked so hard to capture and preserve not only the history of this town, but the spirit of Bindarra Creek. I want to keep that spirit alive, restore the museum to something people will want to visit again, in her honour."

Jack's gaze searched hers, a smile tugged at his mouth that had her heart rate soaring. "No doubt you're the one for the job." He blew out a long breath, reaching out to squeeze her arm. "Thanks for saving Betty."

"You're welcome." Meg ignored the shiver of pleasure that raised goosebumps on her skin as she reached into the back of the ute and pulled out a tow rope. "Take that and tie it around the tow hook on the inner side support bracket of the bumper bar." Handing him one end, she secured the other end around the tow hitch and tightened it. Jack followed her instruction and Meg double-checked all the knots. "We'll drop it off at the garage on the way in, collect all your luggage and then I'll take you to the Riverside Pub."

She climbed back into the ute and waited until Jack gave her the thumbs up from behind the wheel of his car before pulling away.

Jack Hughes was a dangerous threat with that engaging smile and those dimples in his cheeks. He looked and smelled like trouble. A hot, messy, boiling cauldron of trouble.

CHAPTER TWO

*J*ack kept his eyes between the taillights of
the yellow ute and the road while he tried
to keep his mind off the driver.

Meg had dealt with those kids like it was
something she did every day. The same way she'd
handled her aunt in the museum's shop. A soft, natural
control borne out of habit and real affection.

So opposite to Kelsey, hardened by life and her job
as justice correspondent for the major television
network that employed them both. The only thing Meg
and Kelsey had in common was their passion for their
own corner of the world.

But he couldn't let himself be fooled by a
seemingly soft and fuzzy personality again. Tamryn
Hollister had been all sweetness and light too.

Until she'd realised that Jack wasn't interested in
anything more than a story on the current findings of

the Crime and Corruption Commission investigating government front and back benchers for privilege abuse. Then she'd decided to use her own privileges to create a scene.

He'd turned down her offer of a good time. Nicely, he'd thought. In return, she'd leaked a fake sex tape online that had branded him some kind of weird deviant, lost him his job, his girlfriend and his credibility.

The brake lights of the ute lit up and the indicator came on. Jack braked and indicated too. He steered into the parking lot behind Meg's ute.

Gravel crunched under the wheels, sending dust into the air as they rolled to a stop outside an old tin shed with a sign hanging askew above the door, naming it Nobby's Garage.

Through the open doors, he could see a man working under a car on the hoist. Tall, dark hair, rugged, and built like a brick wall.

Meg got out of the ute and closed the door as the man put down his tools and walked out into the sunlight, wiping his hands on a rag. Jack got out too.

"Hey, Meg," the big guy greeted her. "The jobs are piling up. We're going to have to do something soon if Nobby doesn't come back by the end of the month."

"Hi, Jeremy. Yes, I know. I'm working on it. I really appreciate you taking care of the place while Nobby's away. I know you've got your own business to run too."

Jeremy shrugged. "I'll keep doing as much as I can. Looks like you've brought in another one."

"It broke down outside of town. This is Jack Hughes, the owner."

"Pleasure to meet you." Jack stepped forward, hand outstretched as he studied the man. Military. Most likely returned from some war-torn country. They all had that look. Tough. Disciplined. Haunted.

"Jeremy Forster. Nice to meet you too. Jack Hughes, huh? *International Affairs*. I've heard a lot about you." The man's quick grin chased the taciturn expression from his face.

"Yeah?" Jack shook Jeremy's hand. It irked him that now he'd be remembered best for a nasty piece of fake news rather than the legitimate hard work and explosive pieces he'd written.

"You covered that story about corrupt government networks in Afghanistan. The program won you a gold Logie award. Great work, man."

Jack smiled, his shoulders relaxing. "Thanks. It was interesting research."

"Dangerous too, when that research would have taken you right into the middle of the war zone."

"Certainly no playground out there." Jack nodded.

Jeremy shifted on his feet. "Well, let's take a look at the car. What happened?"

"Temperature went up and steam came out from under the bonnet. I pulled over as soon as I could." Jack watched Meg untie the tow rope and roll it up. A smear of dirt on her cheek marred her perfect skin. His fingers itched to reach out and clean it off.

"Good move. Hopefully there won't be any engine damage then." Jeremy moved around the car in easy strides. He stopped at the scarred fender. "Ouch."

Jack drew his gaze away from Meg and back to the car. "Yeah."

"That would have hurt. Are you going to get it fixed?"

Seeing Betty mutilated had hurt more than watching Kelsey walk away with her suitcase in her hand. That's when he'd known it had been over between them long before Tamryn Hollister had appeared on the scene. And Kelsey's reasons for scarring Betty went beyond a viral video. *I've wasted too many years of my life on you, Jack.* "Yeah, I'll get her fixed when I get back to Sydney."

Jeremy nodded. "Good move. She's a beauty."

Meg came to stand between them. "Do you want to get your things together, Jack? I'll give you a lift down to the Riverside Pub."

"Thanks." His feet were so damn sore, all he wanted was a place to put them up and a beer to take the edge off an insane day. He reached in through the window and pulled the key out of the ignition. Opening the boot, he dragged out his suitcase and loaded it into the back of the ute. Then he retrieved his backpack from Betty's passenger seat and handed Jeremy the key. "Take good care of her, mate."

Jeremy grinned. "I'll do my best. See you around."

With a wave, Jack climbed in beside Meg, settling his backpack on the floor between his legs. "Thanks for helping me out."

Meg shrugged as she hot-wired the ute. "It's a pity Nobby isn't here to look after Betty for you."

The sadness in her words made him want to reach for her hand. What the hell was with him today? He wasn't normally a soft touch. Maybe some of the town's craziness was rubbing off on him already. "Why did he go out into the bush?"

Meg turned the ute around on the gravel, waved to Jeremy out the window, and eased her way back onto Main Street. "He thinks he's responsible for Granny Mary's death."

Jack leaned his head back on the headrest and squeezed his eyes shut. Maybe he should have held off on the questions until he'd had that beer and a good night's sleep to clear his head. "What would make him think that? I thought you said she had a heart attack?"

"Granny Mary was recovering from a bout of 'flu. Nobby treated her with his herbs when she insisted that she didn't want to see a doctor for it. When she died, the doctor said the 'flu might have weakened her heart, so Nobby blamed himself for not convincing her to go to the doctor for a 'flu shot."

"It wasn't his fault." He opened his eyes and turned his head toward her, the niggle of a pounding headache returning.

Meg flicked him a glance before turning right and heading for a bridge that crossed a creek. "Everyone accepts that except Nobby."

"But?" Since nothing had been straightforward in this town so far, there had to be a 'but'.

"Grady Flannigan found Melioidosis in his dam a while ago, a soil-borne bacteria which is stirred up by flood waters. It contaminates water and soil, and spreads to humans and animals through contact. Symptoms include pneumonia and septicaemia. Nobby had been camping in the National Park near Grady's dam when Mary fell ill. He'd collected bottles of water from a billabong to boil and brew his herbal teas with."

"So the water in the billabong may have been contaminated and made Mary ill?" Jack's ribs rattled as they crossed a grate on the other side of the bridge.

Meg shrugged. "Maybe. We're waiting on test results to come through. There's been a lot of testing on our water sources since a big storm back in July."

"Put 'flu and contaminated water together and you have a pretty lethal dose." Jack sat straighter, his senses alert. "Your aunt said something about someone wanting to poison the people of Bindarra Creek. Who would have a motive to do that?"

Meg pulled up outside an impressively restored old federation-styled pub. "No one in Bindarra Creek. We've all worked too hard to save the town. Aunty Phyllis has a wild imagination. This was an act of nature, not malice." She sighed into the silence as she disconnected the two wires under the dash and the engine died. "Nobby wouldn't harm Granny Mary."

People committed murder for strange reasons. "What makes you so sure?"

She turned the full strength of her green-blue gaze on him. It made him shift in his seat for reasons that had nothing to do with the current subject and everything to do with thoughts of how sweet her mouth might taste.

"Because he loved her. They never married but they'd promised each other forever. In the outback, that's a lifetime commitment."

"A commitment that ends when one partner dies."

Her eyes flashed angry green fire at him. "Nobby did *not* murder Granny Mary. If you so much as hint that he did when you cover your story, Jack, I'll sue your sorry arse."

Jack grimaced as her words hit his chest like darts on a board. "I'm not that kind of reporter. I like to have all the facts before my stories go to air."

Meg leaned toward him across the space between them, her gaze steady on his, full of promise of retribution. "Then I'll make sure you have your facts straight."

"I can't take you seriously with dirt on your cheek." He reached up to wipe it off with his thumb, her skin warm and smooth under his touch. "There." She shifted under his touch and, reluctantly, he drew his hand away. "I promise to only report the truth, Meg. That's what I do. I don't create sensationalism." Well, he tried not to anyway. The current sensationalism suffocating his reputation had not been of his own making.

Her gaze softened. "I care about these people, this town. We invited your television station here to air a story of hope and survival, to put Bindarra Creek on the map. I don't want anyone hurt in the process. Please don't make Granny Mary a victim when she was a heroine to this town."

She'd leaned so close he could feel her plea whisper across his lips. It made him want to close the gap, press his mouth to hers. But actions like that could get a man into big trouble, and Jack wasn't looking for any more trouble than he was already in. "I promise."

"Hey, guys." A face appeared at Meg's window and they sprang apart, Jack's heart pounding against his ribs. "You must be Jack Hughes. We've been expecting you. I'm Alice."

A cockatoo hopped off the woman's shoulder and pecked at the windscreen wipers. "Alice, Alice, who the fuck is Alice?" The bird tilted its head to give him a one-eyed stare through the glass. "Ooh. Give us a kiss. Give us a kiss."

Meg stifled a giggle, laughter chasing the remaining anger from her eyes. "Jack, meet Alice, our park ranger, and Curly the cockatoo."

He gave Alice a nod and the bird a wary glance. "Hi, Alice. Nice to meet you."

"Come on inside. Dan's waiting to pour you a coldie then I'll show you to your room."

She opened the driver's side door and Meg got out. Jack did the same. He hitched his backpack over his shoulder and reached for his suitcase in the tray of the ute. At least Alice seemed normal. The cockatoo strutted beside him, attacking his shoelaces.

"Curly, stop," warned Alice.

Jack stopped walking. Curly looked at Alice, hopped onto Jack's shoe, pooped on it, and flew away.

Beside him Meg laughed, a full-bodied, magical sound that came from deep inside her and brought a smile to his own lips. "I think you have Curly's stamp of approval," she said between breaths.

Jack eyed his leather shoes, all scuffed and covered in dust from his trek into town, now also stained with bird poop. He briefly wondered why it didn't make him angry that he'd ruined a pair of two-hundred dollar shoes coming to this crazy town.

Jack's smile grew and the dimples it brought to his cheeks deepened. Butterflies stirred in Meg's tummy as his grin transformed his face. Jack Hughes should laugh more often.

Alice nudged her. "Come on inside. I'll give you

something to clean up your shoes, Jack. Dan's looking forward to meeting you."

His shoulders tensed, his expression grew wary and the dimples disappeared. The same reaction he'd had when he'd met Jeremy.

Just how much damage had the scandal arising from that viral video done, not only to his reputation, but to his state of mind? After seeing what his ex-girlfriend had done to his beloved car, Meg couldn't begin to imagine what he'd been through in the past few months.

But as Aunty Phyllis had reminded her before Jack's arrival in town, where there was smoke there was usually fire. And Meg had been burned before by a man with an entrancing smile.

She dragged her attention away from him and focused it on Alice. "Any sign of Nobby today?"

Alice shook her head. "Sorry, Meg. Nothing. I was up in the national park at sunrise, hoping to spot him, but no sign of him at all. Maybe it's time we reported him missing?"

"He'll freak out if the SES come looking for him. He might think they've come to arrest him in connection with the poisoned water. He's already feeling awful about using that billy water to make Granny's tea. We still don't know for sure if it was contaminated or not. Maybe he's gone somewhere else."

"Have you tried his phone?"

"Yes. It goes straight to voicemail." She tried to quell the gut feeling that something bad had happened to Nobby. Worry did strange things to one's mind, created scenarios that might never happen.

Alice started walking toward the pub. "Mm, well, there's been no sign of his old Landcruiser either. Anytime you're ready to start a search, let me know."

Meg rubbed the gooseflesh from her arms. Had it been long enough? The last time Nobby went bush, it took months for him to return. Only Granny Mary knew where he went. She chewed her lip. "I'll have another look through Granny's things to see if she noted where he went before. I've checked her diary and calendar, but there's nothing there."

"I've notified the rangers in the surrounding parks to keep an eye out for him or his vehicle. He would have had to fill up with fuel somewhere."

Meg shook her head. "He always carried enough fuel in jerry cans. He calculates his trips to the last possible litre. He'd have enough fuel to get him to his destination and back."

Alice pushed open the pub door. "I've checked park camera footage in case he's pulled in to one of the parking lots, but there's no sign of him locally. He may have driven a little further out this time. Unfortunately, we won't be able to request road camera footage until we report him missing."

Concern niggled at Meg's thoughts. Nobby had become the grandad she'd never known. And even without blood ties, he was family. She wanted him to come home safely, but not before he was ready.

"Does he go bush often?" Jack's question pulled her from her thoughts.

Meg turned to him. "Every once in a while, he'll take off into the national parks. He loves hiking the trails, studying the wildlife, finding plants, hidden caves. But this time, he just wanted to be alone for a while after Granny's passing. He took her death really hard."

Hadn't they all? Sadness brought the sting of tears to Meg's eyes. Mary had been the much loved backbone of their family. She'd raised Meg after her mum died from cancer far too young, and her father was a stranger whose name they'd never know because that secret had died with her mother.

"What is the longest time Nobby has been gone for?" Jack's gaze held Meg's as she dashed away the dampness from the corner of her eyes.

"A few months. But that was when he came across an ancient cave off a track south of Singleton. He spent weeks out there documenting his find for the museum."

"And got disoriented for a while when he lost sight of his track markers. But he found his way back eventually." Alice ushered them through the door. "Come inside out of the heat. Put your things down behind the bar for now, Jack. Have a drink first." She slipped behind the counter and wrapped her arms around Dan who hugged her back hard.

A pang of longing twisted in Meg's chest. She didn't mind being single, but sometimes she envied the close bond Alice and Dan shared. "Dan, meet Jack Hughes." Beside her, Jack twitched uncomfortably.

Alice's partner smiled broadly as he extended a hand to shake Jack's. "Pleasure to meet you, mate. That story you covered about the Anzacs at Gallipoli was outstanding. Mary recorded it on disc to put in the museum video library."

Jack's breath whooshed out as he shook Dan's hand. "Thank you." He looked at Meg. "Do you still have the recording?"

She smiled. "Of course. Some of the books and magazines were damaged when a water pipe burst in the roof and flooded the shop. We're doing everything we can to rescue them. Luckily, Mary had already put the video collection into the safe, so the old tapes, DVDs and thumb drives were unscathed. We're working on uploading everything to a cloud-based video library."

Dan grinned as he handed Jack a beer, liquid golden amber under a frothy head, moisture coating the glass. "Cheers, mate."

"Cheers." Jack took the beer, eyeing it a little suspiciously. "Where did you say it was brewed?"

Dan chuckled. "Sydney. For now. We've had the all clear on our drinking water supply. There's no sign of contamination. But we're not brewing any ourselves until we've run a little lower on stock. Gives the dust time to settle on rumours."

Meg studied the frown on Jack's face as he lifted the glass to his lips. He'd know all about the damage rumours could do.

His first sip was cautious, his second a full mouthful. A satisfied sigh escaped him before he licked the foam from his top lip. The butterflies in Meg's tummy took flight again as he smiled.

"That's a good drop." Jack held his beer up to the sunlight coming in through the windows, admiring the rich golden colour.

Long fingers with neatly manicured nails circled the pilsener glass, fine dark hair sprinkled across strong forearms that maybe saw a workout or two in his local gym. Meg suspected they led to equally firm biceps and wondered what they looked like under the rolled up sleeves of his business shirt.

White shirt, black jeans, and shoes designed for nightclubs. He bore too many city similarities to Logan, so she ordered the butterflies to settle. Jack Hughes would be gone the minute he completed his story, and that was a good thing. She didn't need to be distracted from restoring the museum and putting it on the must-see tourist map the way Granny Mary had always wanted it to be.

"Well, I guess I'll be getting back to the museum. I can recommend the food here in the pub's bistro, Jack. Dan's mum, Maureen, is an amazing cook. Once you're settled in, I'll be happy to answer any questions you have for your story. There is a new owner over at the local paper too. I'm sure she'll be happy to give you access to the archives."

There, all business. Now all she needed to do was convince herself she didn't like watching his throat work as he swallowed or hearing his sigh of pleasure as he sipped his beer.

His tongue made an appearance again to trace the taste of the ale on his lips. "Thank you, Meg. I appreciate the help." Jack held out his hand to shake hers.

She hesitated for a second before letting her hand be swallowed in his. No matter how strong and warm his hands were, or how stomach-twisting his smile was, she would not fall for Jack Hughes.

CHAPTER THREE

*J*ack had fallen asleep to the muted thump of music down in the bar and he'd woken to the song of the birds this morning. No sirens or traffic noise, not even the occasional sound of a blaring car horn or squeal of a tyre.

He refused to count the annoying tap of the damn cockatoo's beak against his window until Old Man Jake had called Curly to bed sometime around midnight.

Unused to the lack of city noise flirting at the edge of his consciousness, he'd woken once or twice during the night.

Last night, he'd sat in a quiet corner of the bar and studied the people of Bindarra Creek as he'd wolfed down Maureen Molyneaux's epic steak sandwich and curly fries. Old Man Jake had come in with Curly, the cockatoo, to talk to someone named Maki about his pet donkey, Tails.

A small, wiry woman with grey hair down to her waist and wearing flowing purple pants and a bright orange blouse had sat at a table nearby. Her shrewd eyes studied Jack closely. She'd nodded a few times, smiled a knowing smile and then disappeared for a while out the back. When she'd come back inside, Jack could have sworn he'd caught a whiff of sweet-smelling weed.

"Edwina Lette," Alice had informed him as she'd brought him another beer. "Completely harmless. Unless you let her read your palm. She's scarily accurate."

Yep, he'd pass on that one, thank you. What had struck him though, was the camaraderie as people had milled around, come and gone. No doubt about it, he'd landed himself in the middle of a tight-knit community. A place so far removed from the anonymity of inner Sydney nightlife, it had made him feel exactly like the intruder he was.

Disappointment had swelled in his chest as the clock on the wall had ticked off the hours, and Meg hadn't returned to the pub. Yep, he hadn't been able to understand that thought either.

With a breakfast plate piled high with bacon, sausage, eggs and toast in front of him this morning, he tried to convince himself it was only because he'd wanted to find out more from her about the town and the story he was here for.

Dan pulled out a chair and sat. "Sleep okay?"

"Yeah, thanks. A bit quieter around here than I'm used to."

"Not always that quiet. Wait until karaoke night." Dan grinned. "A big change from city life, but it grows on a man."

"You sound like you know what you're talking about." Jack cut into a beef sausage, poked it with his fork and popped it in his mouth. The thought of living in a small town made his feet itch to hit the road.

Dan laughed. "I'm a tree-changer. Left the concrete jungle behind a few years ago, arrived in Bindarra Creek and the rest is history. I wouldn't go back to city life if you paid me a million bucks."

Jack laid his fork on his plate. "Poisoned water, storms, fire, drought, floods, rustlers and a town on the brink of economic collapse. Sounds like a tree-changer's nightmare."

"Ah, that's your reporter's view, Jack. You're looking at an ex A-list investment broker who now owns a re-birthed pub with egg stains on the beer garden wall, stubborn possums in the roof, and a pet kangaroo." Dan shrugged. "Well, actually Muttley thinks we're *his* pets, but still ... Bindarra Creek is so much more than just a small town where a handful of the population resides. If you want to capture the true spirit of this town, you're going to have to look past the obvious."

Jack frowned. "Egg stains?"

"Out of all that you pick the egg story?" Dan grinned. "When I first bought the pub, two young kids looking for trouble chose the side wall to egg. I taught them the right way to throw an egg and then I made them clean the wall. They turned it into a mural instead. Every now and then, they add something new to their artwork. The mural is a talking point, an accurate portrayal of life in Bindarra Creek. The boys are both employed on a farm outside of town, staying out of trouble now."

"In the city, they might have ended up in juvenile detention." Jack shrugged as he picked up his fork again. "Not all stories have a happy ending."

"That's why the residents of Bindarra Creek are trying damn hard to keep this town alive. I hope that's the spirit you'll find to base your story on rather than the disasters that have struck it down."

Unease coiled in Jack's gut. His directive had been to focus on the disasters and turmoils because that's what got bums in seats in front of the screen. No one wanted 'nice' on reality television these days. The more drama and destruction, the higher the ratings.

Jack preferred to report on the truth, a balanced report the way he'd always done it. This time though, his boss wanted dirt because a nice story about a small town coming back to life and a boring old museum wouldn't make the cut.

The possibility of the owner of the museum being poisoned, and a man on the run responsible for giving the poisoned water to her? Now *that* was a story. Add in delinquent teens, weed-smoking psychics, gun-toting roustabouts and potty-mouthed cockatoos? Depending on how the production team portrayed it, Bindarra Creek could end up the laughing-stock of Australia. The thought left a sour taste in Jack's mouth.

He put down his fork again, his appetite fleeing. "I'll do my best to report the truth, Dan. This isn't my usual assignment."

"I've seen your work. I know what you can do. I like you, Jack, but I love this town and the people who live here. If you can't deliver a story devoid of negative sensationalism, I suggest you leave town as soon as your car is good to go, or you might find yourself driven out by a lynch mob. And trust me, you don't want to get on the wrong side of the CWA. Before they'll allow you to leave town, they'll deliver their own kind of punishment. Like the time they made me man the plank in the dunking booth at one of their fundraisers. I can vouch that the water is balls-shrinking cold, and Meg's Aunty Phyllis has a mean and accurate arm." Warning delivered, Dan pushed back his chair and stood.

"Cheers, thanks." Jack watched Dan walk away with a feeling that this story wouldn't be as cut and dried as he'd thought it would be.

A flicker of excitement chased away the churn. For the first time since being given this assignment, he was interested. Interested in what made a successful investment broker move to a dying town, what made a girl as beautiful and intelligent as Meg stay when so many possibilities lay outside the town limits for her. And what about Mary and Nobby? Jack turned his attention back to his plate.

"Freedom." The word came out clipped and decisive from a feminine throat.

Jack's heart dived into his stomach and resurfaced to pound heavily against his ribs. When the hell had Edwina Lette slipped into the seat Dan had vacated? He clasped his hands between his knees to stop them shaking.

"I'm sorry?"

"You will be. There will be many regrets." She smiled and repeated, "Freedom. You like travel and adventure. A man always hanging out for that next big experience. You don't like to put down roots which is why you love your job. It gives you freedom."

He wanted to correct her. He used to love his job until it got him into trouble with a prominent politician's daughter. "That's pretty much a requirement, isn't it? To love your work?"

She leaned forward, elbows on the table, head cocked to one side, clear eyes studying him so hard he could almost feel her peeling away the layers from his soul. "You're the life and soul of the party, and that's what got you into trouble. You're an attractive package, Jack Hughes. Hard to resist. You're Peter Pan on steroids and no flighty Tinkerbell will ever tie you down. You're a life number five. And I know the perfect seven for you."

"I'm not looking for the perfect seven, Mrs Lette." The thought alone made his head thump. Been there. Done that. Betty wore the scars as the reason he should never go there again. "And with all due respect to you, I don't believe in astrology."

"It's *Ms* Lette but you can call me Edwina. I'm talking numerology, young man. The number seven I see likes her own time for reflection and doesn't mind being alone in her own space. She won't tie you down, but be warned, she won't ask you to stay either. So think carefully before you leave." She paused to look a little harder. So hard a shiver trickled down Jack's spine and he swore he could feel the sensation of pins and needles behind his eyes. "Yes. You'll be good together. If you allow the truth to guide your heart." Edwina held out her hand. "Give me your palm."

"Not a chance."

Her wicked chuckle filled the gap across the table. "Afraid of what I might see?"

Reluctantly, Jack let her take his hand and turn it palm up. What harm could it do? It was all mumbo-jumbo anyway. He'd been accused of a lot of things in his time but being afraid wasn't one of them.

She traced his lifeline with the tip of her finger and Jack shifted, uncomfortable with the weird sensations prickling his skin. "Your life has travelled many different paths, Jack. Some have brought fulfillment, others haven't." Her eyes met his, her scarily penetrating gaze drawing him in. "The path you're on now is the right one."

He withdrew his hand as she released it. "That's reassuring to know, thanks."

Edwina chuckled. "We'll talk again in a few days, but for now I've seen why Mary trusted you with her story, and that's enough for me." She slapped her hand down on the table and pushed herself up off the chair. "Have a nice day, Jack Hughes."

Edwina floated off on a cloud of spicy perfume to the clink and rhythm of jiggling bracelets, leaving him feeling a little spooked. Jack stared at his half-full plate, no longer hungry.

He hadn't known Mary Moonie from a bar of soap, had never met or talked to the woman, so Edwina's talk about her trusting him made no sense at all. Crazy, delusional, rubbishy guesswork that made him decidedly uncomfortable. He lined up his knife and fork on the plate, his belly churning.

"Would you like me to warm that up for you, love?" Dan's mum, Maureen, appeared beside him.

"No thanks, Mrs Molyneaux, I've had enough. But it was delicious, thank you."

She reached for the plate. "I hope Edwina didn't spoil your appetite with her predictions?"

He smiled and shrugged off the weird feeling that the old lady really had penetrated his mind. "It's all good, thanks. I promise to do dinner justice."

Maureen returned his smile. "Perfect." She turned

to walk away as Meg rushed in through the door. "Ah, good morning, Meg."

"Morning, Maureen," she said as they passed each other, then stopped at his table. "Hey, Jack."

All Jack could manage was a nod. For the second time since meeting her, she'd stolen his breath away. Meg Moonie was the kind of ethereal beauty a man needed to reach out to touch to make sure she was real, and not some outback legendary creature blown into town on the breeze. A man would have to be dead not to react to her beauty and presence, and Jack was by no means dead. Only wary.

He found his tongue. "Meg."

She handed him a takeaway cup. "Real Greek coffee, compliments of the Levonis family at the Cyprus Café. You've been invited to go and taste the best baklava in Bindarra Creek."

"I'll be sure to stop by for some later, thank you." Jack nodded as he took the cup and sniffed the aroma leaking from the lid. "That does smell like a great brew."

"Only the best beans make it into the grinder at the café." Meg smiled down at him.

Remembering his manners, Jack stood to pull out a chair for her. "Would you like to sit? Can I order you something to eat?"

Meg shook her head. "No, thank you. I've just been out to the McGregor farm, so I've got a lot to unload.

Craigellachie was full of treasures Angus could generously donate to the museum."

"Do you receive a lot of donations?" Standing up had brought him closer to her. He could smell the scent of soap and perfume mixed with the tang of old rust.

"The community have been very generous in helping me restore the museum. Come by when you're done and I'll show you around."

"I will, thank you." A timely reminder of the reason he'd come to town. "I might stop in at the Cyprus Café on the way to thank them for the coffee."

Her smile triggered a tumble of attraction somewhere below his sternum. "I think the family would like that very much. We have a lot of good people in this town who look out for each other, and they're all dying to meet you. See you later."

As she walked away with a wave, Jack didn't doubt that at all. Near the bar stood Dan, Alice, Old Man Jake, Grandad Charlie and Curly, all pretending not to watch his interaction with Meg.

Already he could see the residents pulling together as they sussed him out. Before the fake video went viral, no one had ever questioned his credibility. He had to get this story right to claw that back. He just wasn't sure how he would achieve that stuck in a dying town that clung stubbornly to the dream of survival.

~

Meg sifted through the items donated by Angus McGregor. Branding irons, a few rusty old farm tools and a butter churn that would need very little restoration. Craigellachie's owner might as well have handed her gold. Each item had a story to tell.

She picked up a branding iron and ran her fingertip along the shaft. Granny Mary would have said she could feel the spirit of the stockmen who'd used it still present in the metal. Meg wished she'd inherited Mary's power to see into the past, instead she'd have to rely on the memories of the people and any stories the CWA ladies could tell.

The bagpipes caught her eye, and she smiled at the thought of the early McGregors dancing to their tune in the family tartan the way they'd danced in the framed photo Angus had dropped onto the pile. So many happy memories immortalised forever.

A shiver crept up her spine. When she'd approached the television station to do a story on Mary and the museum, she'd meant for it to be a feel-good piece that would boost interest and tourism to the town they'd all worked so hard to rebuild. But now that Jack was here, doubts niggled.

He was a hard-nosed reporter who'd seen things no one should ever see. His programs were diverse, hard-hitting and action-filled. A sleepy hollow like Bindarra Creek was far removed from the war zone in Afghanistan and the dog-eat-dog political scenes inside the walls of Parliament House. How much interest would he really have in the history of an old town? Could Granny Mary have been wrong about him?

Aunty Phyl tapped on the wooden door frame of the workshop out the back of the museum. "Jack's here."

Time to find out. She turned from the sorting table to greet him. "Hello, again. I hope you slept well last night?"

Gone were the collared shirt and nightclub shoes from the day before. This morning he wore a dark blue T-shirt that hugged a body it was a sin to hide under a fancy dress shirt. No saggy pants for Jack. His blue denim jeans fit the way they were designed to, lovingly clinging to long legs and trim hips. Today's footwear was a pair of tan hiking boots, scuffed from adventures unknown.

He smiled that absent smile that would have anyone susceptible between age five to a hundred melting to the floor in a puddle. "Once Curly stopped calling to me outside my window, yes."

Meg's heart tripped as his green eyes searched hers. "I think Curly has a crush on you."

Aunty Phyl snorted and rolled her eyes. "That bird has strange tastes."

Meg looked over Jack's shoulder to shoot her a warning look. "Play nice, Phyl. I think I hear the shop bell?"

"I think that's wishful thinking, but I can take a hint." She turned away from the door. "Behave yourself alone with my niece, Hughes. I've got eyes on you." Phyl pointed to the security camera on the corner of the workshop, and then she was gone.

Amusement lit his eyes. "Your aunt is a character."

"She's the best. Phyl has a heart of gold, so she means well. Don't let her fool you with that tough exterior. Underneath it, she's a marshmallow." Meg turned away to place the forgotten branding iron onto the table. "Where would you like to start, Jack?"

His presence filled her space as he wandered over, rubber-soled boots silent on the concrete floor. Leaning a hip against the table, he folded his arms and faced her. "Let's start with what you're doing in here."

Safe, neutral ground. "This is the sorting table. After the storm and the fires, I put out a call for donations to the museum. With all the big clean-ups around the place, I knew there might be some things of historical value about to be thrown away or recycled. I've collected everything from these branding irons to an old seeder for some new displays. But a lot of the items need to be cleaned up and restored first."

Meg winced. He'd definitely be bored to tears if she rambled on. Why on earth had she thought this would be a good idea? Could he really put together a newsworthy story out of a pile of old abandoned items and a town that had emerged from the ashes of fire and flood? A story about a woman so strong that, without her, Meg felt like her world had crumbled to nothing.

So here she was, trying to breathe life into Mary's

dream and in some way, to bring her granny back to life.

Jack's arm brushed hers as he reached for a rusty item on the table, sending pleasant tingles skittering across her skin. "What's this?"

Heat rushed into Meg's cheeks. What was it about Jack that had her heart skipping beats and her tummy doing swallow dives at a hint of a smile? Hadn't she learned her lesson after Logan? Reporters couldn't be trusted. And she'd invited this one into their tight-knit community to delve into their past. She had to trust him to tell their story in the spirit of the town and now she wasn't so sure he would do that.

Second thoughts silenced the swallows flapping their wings of attraction. "It's an old horn saw from the eighteen hundreds. Cattle were either dehorned or the pointy edges removed to reduce risk of injury to handlers and other cattle during muster and transport. These days, it's a heavily controlled practice because of animal welfare concerns, but horns can cause a lot of damage and bruising in a herd."

"I'd imagine it would be a pretty nasty experience for the animal." He moved the tool around in his hands. "Would you leave the horn saw in its original condition?"

Meg shrugged, trying not to stare at his hands. Big, strong, beautiful hands with long fingers. "I'd clean up the blade a little with some white vinegar and maybe a little orange oil on the wooden handle to help preserve it, but mostly I think it tells a story exactly as it is."

He looked up from the blade, his eyes capturing hers, the flutters in her belly returning. "And what story would that be?"

Meg pressed a hand to her stomach to settle the churn, sadness returning to fill the space. "Granny Mary was really good at seeing the story behind the objects in the museum." She paused to study Jack's face, searching for something that would confirm he would take Mary's powers seriously and not laugh them off.

Jack tipped his head to the side, cocked an eyebrow and offered her an encouraging smile. "How?"

The words rushed out, tumbling over each other. If she said them quickly, he might believe it. "Mary had second sight. She could see into the past and the future. If she touched objects in the museum, she'd pick up vibrations and have visions of the people who'd held them and receive insight into their life stories."

The tug of his mouth held a touch of scepticism. "As a reporter, I prefer to deal in hard facts, but I'm listening."

"Listening isn't enough. You need to feel it, Jack." Meg pushed away from the table and folded her arms across her chest. "I think it's time I showed you around the place. Starting with the cellar."

CHAPTER FOUR

*M*eg walked ahead of him across the crumbling courtyard, back into the museum. Excitement trickled into his blood as he recognised the familiar thirst to gain information and facts.

He didn't believe in the paranormal, but museums had always made his skin itch. As if the footprints of the past had left behind transient energy.

Closing the back door behind him, he concentrated on Meg's soft voice as she launched into the history of Mary's museum.

"Born in 1946, Mary arrived in Australia from England as a toddler in late October 1948. Her father, a World War II soldier, joined the post-war migrant boom, took advantage of the assisted passage scheme, and brought his family across the world to begin a new life."

"A ten-pound Pom."

"Essentially, yes. He found work as a brickie here in Bindarra Creek as the town went through a growth spurt. In December 1949, Aunty Phyllis was born." Meg led Jack down a set of sturdy concrete steps and stopped four steps down. She pointed to a gemstone set into the brick wall. "Mary placed that moonstone in the wall to mark the death of her parents in a car accident in 1963."

"Why a moonstone?" Jack crouched down to examine the pale, almost transparent stone where it shimmered in the low lighting from the bunker lights on the walls.

"This is an Albite moonstone from Canada. Mary inherited her gift from her mother who, like Edwina Lette, had psychic powers. It's said that the moonstone has the power to reunite lovers, so Mary placed the stone as a symbol of hope that her parents would be reunited in the after-life and remain together forever."

Jack ran his fingers over the smooth surface of the stone. Energy pulsed in through his fingertips, travelled up his arm and kick-started his heart. He snatched his hand back and jumped to his feet. "I think you might have some stray current running through that wall, Meg. You might want to get an electrician to check it out."

Meg smiled. "That's not electricity, Jack. That's magic." She continued down the steps. "In the summer of 1965, when Mary was just nineteen, a young Irishman named Carrick Kenny came to town. He and Mary fell in love, married and opened up a general store, stocking everything from dress material to compost. But Carrick loved his horses, gambling and whiskey, and Mary struggled to keep the business afloat."

She stopped suddenly and Jack, his gaze on the coloured patterns on the ceiling of the stairwell, crashed into her back. His arms snaked around her waist and pulled her back against his chest to stop her toppling down the remaining stairs.

"Oops! Sorry. Are you okay?" he said, his heart pounding against her warm back. Apple-scented shampoo mixed with musk and jasmine to create a tantalising perfume that teased his nostrils.

"I'm okay," she replied. Her back rose and fell against him as she breathed deeply.

For a moment, Jack enjoyed the feeling of her against him. Soft, warm, electric — a charged connection that heated his blood and made his hands itch to explore her curves, her hair, her lips, her face.

He dropped his arms from around her and took a step back. What was he thinking? Jack Hughes — bachelor supreme — was free to go wherever the road led. Roaming international correspondents didn't put down stakes.

Women were hard work and some, more

importantly, were troublemakers. And thanks to one such boldly flirtatious girl, he'd be roaming to backwater towns like this one for a very long time if he couldn't find a way out.

But his boss didn't want happy-ever-after stories of reunited dead lovers, or museum owners with magic powers. He wanted high-powered, hard-hitting journalism that would erase that damn dirty viral video from the public's minds. And if Jack wanted his job back, he'd have to deliver.

He pushed away the sensory memory of Meg in his arms, and the tug he'd felt toward her. She didn't belong there. In his arms. In his mind. In his life. She was small town. He was big city. Worlds apart. "We should move on."

Meg cleared her throat and skipped down two steps ahead of him. "In 1975, Mary's marriage to Carrick collapsed. He left Bindarra Creek and moved to Sydney, leaving Mary pregnant and alone with a failing business to run." She pointed to the roof. "To indicate a new start in her life, Mary created a border of moonstones around the door to protect her and her daughter. My mother."

Jack looked up and followed the arch the moonstones created around the entry to the cellar. Had Meg felt that connection that pulsed between them? Was that why her breath still came in soft, uneven falls? Weird, he'd never felt that kind of zap before. "She really loved her moonstones," he said, trying to distract his thoughts from the feeling of her in his arms.

As they walked through the archway, the same pulsing energy he'd felt earlier when running his hands over the moonstone flowed through him. Except this time, it was stronger, creating a sense of peace in him he hadn't felt for a very long time. Cynicism had become his master in the big bad world of reporting, there'd been no time for peace and dreams.

"Yes, she completely believed in their power too. Moonstones were Mary's tool of choice for looking into the future. She had an affinity with them she inherited from her mother."

"Like looking into a crystal ball?" The cynic in Jack's heart tried hard to break through the haze of magic.

Meg laughed, a sound that trickled through him and set his blood on fire. "No, not at all. Moonstones enhance intuition. Mary had a gift that allowed her to see the true nature of a person from a picture, a smile or a handshake. She saw beyond the outer shell and into their souls. By creating this archway, she believed it would bring good fortune and success in business, as well as love, to all who passed through it. She was right. She dedicated the back rooms of the shop to a museum and started collecting memorabilia from all over town. In the cellar, she created a happy haven for herself where she worked with her crystals, creating jewellery and sometimes doing readings with Edwina for those who were interested. Business boomed and love bloomed all over town."

"That might have had more to do with timing than magic." He was pretty sure of that since his research on the town had shown employment growth in the seventies before dwindling again after a massive flood in 1985.

"For Mary, everything was touched by magic. The day before she died, she gave me a moonstone. In it, she said she'd seen my future." Meg raised a hand to her neck and touched the stone that nestled in the vee of her shirt. It shimmered, transparent in the low lighting of the room.

Jack felt the zing between them, a charge so strong it made his fingers tingle and his feet itch to run. "I think you've got the wrong person for this assignment."

"I never chose you. Mary did." Meg let go of her necklace.

"Well that's just crazy. How could she? She died six weeks ago and I was only given this assignment a few days ago." What kind of a psycho den had he walked into?

Meg laughed. "Oh, Jack, if only you could see your face! Sorry, I didn't mean to freak you out. We might be a small town that barely features on Google Maps but for the most part, we're all perfectly sane, I promise." She reached out to touch his arm, her fingers cool on his skin. "You covered a story on the mysterious Venn family and a diamond in their collection."

"The curse of the Kimberley Star." Mockery edged his smile. "The diamond that drove lovers apart and sentenced Venn women to a life of loneliness and bad luck in love. The real story there was that the diamond was stolen by one of Kimberley Venn's many lovers and sold on the black market. He bought shares in the stock market with the proceeds of the sale and became a New York multi-billionaire."

"You questioned the existence of magic and true love, the viability of the curse. Mary liked your reporting style but she thought you needed a lesson in love and reality, and she believed you'd find those things here in Bindarra Creek."

"I don't believe in love. Nothing lasts forever. People change. The dynamics of a relationship change. Once the initial rush of attraction fades, it leaves bitterness in its place." He took in the beauty of her face, the seriousness in her eyes. "It's not magic, it's lust. And when lust fades, what's left to keep a relationship going?"

"Well, maybe that's what Mary wanted you to find out. She wanted you to look inside your heart and find out where the real Jack Hughes was hiding."

Jack scoffed and changed the subject. Enough about love, magic and hearts. He needed a story. "What's with the paintings on the ceilings?"

Meg smiled sadly as she lifted her face to the decorated space. "Mary called them her version of Dreamtime stories. They capture the happiness of every success, every dream, and the sadness of each loss and struggle throughout her lifetime." She pointed to a section of the painting showing a young angel holding a baby. "My mother died not long after I was born. She developed a rare form of blood cancer while she was pregnant with me."

"I'm really sorry to hear that." Jack reached out to squeeze her hand and found he liked the warmth of her skin against his. Too much, so he let her fingers slip away.

"Thank you. Granny Mary and Aunty Phyl kept her alive in my memories. I had a great childhood being raised by them and the people in this town. In Bindarra Creek, we're one big family." She turned to him and smiled. "And just like all families, there are feuds and dramas, but when it comes to the crunch, we all stick together."

"It must have been a shock for you when Mary passed."

"She wasn't done living yet. There was so much she still wanted to do. But she'd run out of funds as our town started to die. Natural disasters aside, there weren't enough jobs to keep the people here and with very little to lure visitors to the town, we don't get much attention from the outside world. Mary was living off a meagre pension. Then a few years ago, Dodge's wife, Tessa, arrived and obtained a grant for the town to rebuild."

"And Mary had her second chance."

"Not quite. For the most part, it helped us rebuild where we needed to. The grant didn't extend to the museum, unfortunately, and Mary wasn't successful in her application for a heritage grant from the Royal Australian Historical Society."

"And that's why you called the station?"

Meg nodded, her gaze pleading. "I thought if viewers could see how much this town means to the community, it might help when I lodge the next application. I want to keep Mary's dream alive, Jack. Her dream, and the dreams of everyone else in this town. Bindarra Creek is more than just a town. It's a living, breathing, beating heart."

Even as the words left her lips, the rush of love for Bindarra Creek filled her heart. How could an outsider, a city boy like Jack understand how much the survival and rebirth of the town had meant to the families whose history had been woven into its existence for almost a hundred and eighty years?

Dropping her gaze from his, she moved away from him. Here, in Mary's sanctuary, surrounded by her imprint on life, the doubts surged in Meg's mind again as she wondered if she'd made a mistake bringing him down here. Would he see the essence of Mary's being or would he only see eccentricity?

Jack looked around the room, touching things,

studying them carefully, reading the old newspaper clippings framed on the wall. Mary's more personal memories that had made the local newspaper on carnival day.

His size made the room feel smaller, the ceiling lower than normal in the cellar. His strength seemed to fill the space and command it, own it, drawing her closer.

Logan had not been allowed past the cellar door. Mary had said he disturbed the aura of the room and would leave a negative imprint that would take too much energy to cleanse. Meg wondered how Mary would feel about Jack.

A pang of sadness curled in her chest. She'd scoffed at Granny's fears about Logan, yet Mary had been proved right about him. Meg would give anything right now for some guidance about Jack. To know for sure whether letting him poke about in the essence of their community had been such a good idea after all.

But she needed that grant badly to keep the museum going, and the only way to do that was to put Bindarra Creek on the map.

"What are these?" Jack picked up a box of cards.

"Fairy cards."

In his big hands, the cards looked small, insignificant, yet Meg knew just how big a punch they could pack when someone dealt a card that hit home with an uncannily accurate message. She doubted Jack would believe in their magic or accuracy. He was too much of a realist.

"How do they work?" He took a step closer, the distance between them narrowing.

"Through the power you transmit into them. Basically, you shuffle the pack a few times so your energy is left on the deck. Any cards that fall out while you're shuffling are meant for you regardless. When you're done shuffling, you pick out as many cards as you feel drawn to."

Jack turned the box over and studied the back. "They come with a book to interpret each card. Isn't that cheating?" His blue gaze pinned hers, full of scepticism.

"The book is only a guide for interpretation. You're drawn to the card you need, and the meaning will bring a personal message for you to interpret and apply."

"Sounds a little dodgy to me." He turned the box over again. "Can you read the cards, Meg?"

"I don't have Granny Mary's gift, but I've used them a few times for myself." Once she'd been done crying wasted tears over Logan and had started to feel less numb from his betrayal. "Would you like to try?" Meg waited for the scoff, the brush off, the look that would tell her he thought she was nuts.

Instead, he surprised her with a shrug. "Why not? I've got nothing to lose. A little bit of fun never hurt anybody."

"Okay then." Meg held out her hand for the deck. "I'll cleanse them first so that there's no residual trace from the last user."

Which had been Meg. She'd had to dry her tears from the cards when they'd promised so much for the future. And now her tears were because the promises had yet to be fulfilled.

His fingers brushed hers as he handed the box to her, his skin warm against hers. And right there was that tug of attraction that sent the blood bubbling through her veins.

Unsettled by his closeness, she waved a hand to a chair at the reading table. "Have a seat."

Meg took the one opposite him, opened the box and tipped out the cards. She knocked three times on the deck, shuffled them and fanned them out on the table before running a clear crystal across the top, the way Mary had taught her.

Conscious of Jack's gaze on her face, she raised her eyes to his. The intensity in his look triggered the butterflies in her belly. Why was he looking at her like that? She cleared the sudden constriction in her throat.

"Are you sure you want to do this, Jack?"

He dropped his gaze to the cards and shifted on the chair. "Sure. Let's do it." His voice came out gruff as he stretched out long legs and tugged at the denim that hugged his thighs.

Meg gathered the cards into a neat pile before

placing the deck in front of him. "Knock three times on the deck then shuffle the cards well. If any fall out, place them face down on the table. While you shuffle, think of any questions you'd like to ask the spirit guides."

Jack followed her instructions, caught three cards that fell out and chose another three from the top of the deck. "What do I do now?"

Meg swallowed against a dry throat. Watching Jack's hands work the cards brought to mind how they would feel against her skin. "Leave them all face down and turn them over as we go."

A seventh card slipped from the top of the deck as he put it to one side. "This one too?"

Meg nodded. "If it fell from the deck, you're meant to see it."

He laid them out in the sequence they'd been chosen, a smile hovering on his lips. Damn it, why did Jack Hughes have to be so freaking hot when he smiled?

Jack turned over the first card he'd drawn and pressed a long finger onto it. "What does this mean?"

"Let go. What are you holding onto? It could be the past, or it could be control of a situation. Once you let go of what it is that is holding you back, you will attract what you truly desire."

The grin he gave her was so cheeky it fizzed her blood, curled her toes and had heat flushing into her face. "Turn over the next card ... that one means that you're finished with a part of your old life and a new, even more fulfilling life is beginning."

He scoffed at that one. "Certainly can't get any worse."

"That's all part of the first card, Jack. Your new life can't begin until you let go of the old hurt." Meg had drawn those cards too. Letting go hadn't been as easy as the deck had made it sound. "What's next?"

"Perfect timing."

"Ah, that one means the timing is right to move forward. It speaks in harmony with your first two cards. The time is right to let go of the past and start a new life." Unease crawled across her skin as she looked at the next card he'd flipped over.

Jack grinned. "New career. Hallelujah to that. I hope that means a new assignment far away from here." His grin slipped as he looked up at Meg.

She tried not to take it personally. Bindarra Creek wouldn't have been high on his list of chosen assignments. She'd known that. He probably couldn't wait to shake their dust from his boots. Still, the jab hurt when it shouldn't.

"Looks like you'll get your wish. Your career is set to shift in a positive, new and successful direction."

Just like Logan, it would make no sense for someone as successful as Jack to hang around a small town miles from the action in big cities.

Jack flipped over the fifth card and laughed out loud. A deep laugh that crept up from his belly and escaped from his throat. It brought a smile to Meg's lips.

"What's so funny?"

"Love life? It says my love life is about to change for the better." Cynicism fell from his tongue on a dry note. "It hasn't been roses and champagne so far."

"An interesting card considering it relates directly to a question you've asked while shuffling. What exactly did you ask for, Jack?"

"I didn't ask for anything." He picked up the next card, studied it. "Children? Oh, hell no. That's not going to happen."

Meg brushed away the picture in her head of Jack with three kids. Two girls and a boy, born close together. The girls holding hands and skipping along beside him while he carried the boy on his shoulders. The way she'd seen in magazines and online. The pictures of the children in her head bore too close a resemblance to her and Jack.

"It doesn't necessarily mean you'll *have* kids. It could also mean that children are meant to be part of your work or your life's purpose. Do you have nephews and nieces?"

Jack shook his head. "Nope. I'm an only child. My parents are missionaries in Africa."

Meg tapped a finger on her chin. "Mmm ... Well, I'm sure that one will become clear as time progresses. What's your last card?"

Jack placed the children card on top of his

discarded ones. The last card made him push back his chair and stand so suddenly Meg drew in a startled breath.

"Okay, enough of this bullshit."

"You're afraid of marriage, Jack?" That she felt disappointed by the thought didn't make any sense either. Sure, he was a good-looking guy and as sexy as all hell, but he was a player not a stayer.

"Even more than I am of children." He gathered up the cards and placed them back in the box. "What's next on the grand tour?"

Meg eased out of the chair, placing the clear crystal on top of the card box as she stood. The crystal would help clear whatever residual energy the cards held that had spooked Jack.

"I'll take you through the old storeroom where the museum first started. Perhaps after that you could take a stroll around town and get to know the locals? Did you pop into the Cyprus Café?"

"Yes, I met the whole family, and promised I'd go back there for lunch later. I could get hooked on their coffee."

"Wait until you try Thalia's baklava. It's addictive." Meg didn't want to think about the rush of relief that Thalia was so in love with Kel Jones, she wouldn't notice Jack. Men loved women who could bake and cook, and Thalia thrived on her Greek-given gift. "Right, well ... let's go upstairs then."

Meg led the way up with Jack close to her back and

energy coming off him in waves. Whatever it was the cards had shown him had him rattled. He might not have asked the spirit guides for anything outright, but she couldn't help pondering on what question he'd had hidden in his heart.

CHAPTER FIVE

*J*ack wished it was closer to beer o'clock as he watched Meg's slim hips sway up the stairs ahead him. Greek coffee may not be strong enough to drown the fear those cards had put into him. They'd cut too damn close to the bone for comfort.

The career thing he could still swallow. Marriage? Children? A new love in his life? No way. Promises of happy-ever-after were not for him. Kelsey had known that.

They'd always been career-focused, their relationship coming second to ambition. A switch that had flipped with the arrival of the viral video and Tamryn Hollister on the scene.

Perhaps Kelsey had wanted more, but anything more than a few days in each other's company had almost driven them both to murder. Their casual, drop-in relationship had suited their needs and their careers. Until it ended the way it had and then he'd wondered briefly if perhaps he'd got it all wrong. Maybe Kelsey had been a forever kind of girl. Either way, he wasn't a forever guy.

Jack shook the thoughts free from his head as he passed the moonstone embedded into the wall. Fairy tales and magic were for dreamers and he dealt in reality. He'd been raised in a boarding school while his parents travelled the wilds of Africa rescuing other people's children, oblivious to the needs of their own child.

He didn't resent their calling, but because of it he knew nothing of family life or parenting. He only knew discipline, punishment and how to survive the dark halls of realism. Of accepting a situation and dealing with it. Meg's Granny Mary would have a field day if she was still alive and could look inside his head.

At the top of the stairs, Meg turned to the left, leading the way through a door into a room much bigger than he'd expected for an old storeroom.

"The original shop was built back in 1842 when Bindarra Creek was little more than a staging depot. New settlers began arriving in the area in 1839. The town grew, and more storage was needed for supplies for them as well as horses and travellers between Armidale and Moree. Hence the size of the storage room."

Jack looked around, taking in the rusty brown

stains of water damage on the walls and ceiling. Old wallpaper curled and peeled at the corners, ready to drop off the wall. Piles of books, clothing, linen and God knew what else were stacked high on tables. A damp, musty, stale smell hung in the air and made Jack want to throw open the old sash windows to let in some fresh air.

Meg must have picked up on his intentions because she said, "The windows are swollen shut. As soon as we have some extra funds, I can get a carpenter in to refurbish or replace them. We did our best to save as much of the inventory as possible by putting things above the water level, but unfortunately, the stock still took a hammering."

"How much of it can be saved?"

"Most of it. But there's a lot of work to be done. Dodge Myers helps me out with some of the furniture restoration, and the CWA have started freshening up the old clothes as best they can. It takes care and time because the materials are so old and fragile. Some just simply fall apart." Meg reached across a table piled with books to pull out an old photograph album. "This is what the museum looked like before the fires, floods and storms we've had in recent years. The town has taken a battering, and that makes us all the more determined to rebuild what has been destroyed."

Jack stood closer as Meg opened the album. Her scent mingled with the smell of old paper. Sepia changed to black and white then colour as photography progressed through the ages on the page. Fragile tissue paper separated the album pages, protecting the photographs from damage.

He listened as she told the story behind a few and skipped over others. He'd thought he'd be bored flipping through the town's history, but he could listen to the lilt in Meg's voice all day. She had a storyteller's voice, an undiscovered gift. Jack wondered if she'd audition for a voice-over position at the station.

"Have you ever thought about letting it all go, Meg? It seems like restoration is going to be a money pit. What about insurance?"

Meg closed the album and put it back on the table. "Granny Mary couldn't afford to keep up the payments. I tried my best to help. I offered to move to the city, find a better job so I could send money. But Granny knew I'd hate it away from here. Each year, I watched the town die a little more. Until Tessa got that grant and we had the opportunity to grow again. That gave us all hope." She turned to look at him, her gaze steady on his. "This town, the museum ... it's my life. It's the only place I ever want to be because it's everything I am."

Jack's throat tightened at the love in her words, his inner cynic seeking out humour to stop him from reaching for her and folding her close. "Old, dusty and smelly?"

She laughed, but he spotted the movement of her finger dashing away a tear from under her eye. "Funny, Jack."

"This place means a lot to you."

"It means the world to me. Help me save Mary's dream. Please. It's all I have left of her."

Jack swallowed the lump in his throat. *Fuck it.* He drew her into his arms and held her tight. He'd been in war zones, third world countries and political circuses around the world, but nothing had touched his heart quite like this girl, stranded out in the arse-end of nowhere, keeping dreams alive.

"I'll do my best." His best was all he had. He lifted her chin, ran his thumb across the dampness on her cheeks and struggled against the urge to kiss her.

Her green eyes shone with tears as they searched his. "Thank you." Her lips parted on a sigh, so temptingly close to his.

The air thickened between them, charged with sudden tension that had him drawing her closer, reluctant to release her just yet. And when that invisible connection brought their faces closer together, Jack found himself powerless to resist. He kissed her, gently at first, a touch of his lips to hers that led to a journey of slow exploration and discovery. When she returned his kiss and relaxed in his arms, her hands flat against his chest, trapped between them, he kissed her harder, deeper.

Her taste embedded itself in his senses, seeped into his memory and lodged itself in his mind.

He tugged her shirt out of her shorts, lifted it so he could feel her skin again his hands. Her body curved to fit his perfectly, moulded into him, touching in all the right places in a way that made him wish for more. That he could take her to bed and love her with his body and soul.

He balled his fists around the hem of her shirt, crumpling the material in his grip. Meg wasn't a streetwise lover. She was a girl with a heart that would get broken because she didn't play games. He'd eventually leave town to go home to the city and she'd stay behind. In the same way she'd told him Carrick had left Mary. Just not pregnant, because he was smarter than that.

Jack eased away slowly. Reluctant to leave the comfort of her mouth, he dropped tiny kisses on her lips before tucking her head under his chin, holding her loosely so she could leave at any time.

Time stood still in the musty room, their heartbeats hammering in the silence, until a shrill whistle pierced the air.

"Meg!" Aunty Phyllis' shout followed the whistle.

Meg groaned into Jack's chest, before stepping out of his arms. "In here," she called.

Jack moved away, his back to the door. While his common sense said the interruption was for the best, it would take a few minutes for his body to register that a kiss was as good as it would get.

Phyllis appeared in the doorway and he turned his head to greet her. Her sharp gaze bounced between them, her mouth pulling tight. "Riley Morgan is here to see you. To see us. In his official capacity as senior sergeant." She shot a look at Jack. "I'm not sure he should be there."

"We've got nothing to hide, Aunty Phyl."

"I'm not so sure about that." She turned away to walk back down the hallway, her plastic heels scuffing against the floorboards. "And tuck your shirt back in, missy, or the whole town will know you've been necking with the reporter."

"I'm not ... I wasn't ..." Meg looked at Jack.

A chuckle stuck in his throat, turning to a choke when Aunty Phyllis said, "I might be old and going blind, but I can still spot a man trying to hide a hard-on a mile away. Get your arses into the front shop as soon as you're both decent. Riley's champing at the bit."

Meg's heart filled with trepidation as she approached the front shop with Jack close behind her. She tried to soothe her thoughts. This was Bindarra Creek, the cops dropped by for coffee or tea and a chat. It didn't necessarily mean bad news.

Riley stood at the counter, his usual relaxed stance

replaced by a stiff spine and spread feet as if he expected her to go on the attack. "Hi, Meg."

"Hi, Riley. This is Jack Hughes from Channel Eight. Jack, meet Senior Sergeant Riley Morgan. What's up?" Meg's tummy churned a little harder. If it had been something minor, he would have sent his senior constable, Abby Taylor, or even the young probie, AJ. But when Riley Morgan showed up himself, he meant business.

"We've got the toxicology reports. Finally. Don't know why it takes so bloody long to get them back." He looked at Jack. "Is it okay to talk?"

"It's fine. There'll be no secrets from Jack."

Riley eyed him warily. "It's not like it will be a secret with all the testing going on. The good news is that the water Nobby had in his billy was cleared of Melioidosis. As have all the billabongs and dams in the immediate area. The water is clean."

Relief flooded Meg. "That's good news, right?"

"Depends on which side of the fence you're on." He swiped the screen on his tablet. "Testing did find large traces of oleander in the dregs of Mary's cup."

Meg's tummy dropped like a stone. "But that's ..."

"Listed on the register as a toxic plant material. Although it does have limited medicinal qualities, it has a history of being used as a suicide aid." Riley tucked his tablet under his arm. "Meg, if you know something, now's a good time to tell me."

"Nobby wouldn't hurt Mary. He's not like that."

Cold shivers raised gooseflesh on Meg's arms. "It could have been in the water already."

Riley shook his head. "The only sample that tested positive was the herbal tea out of Mary's mug. Meg, unless I can find a good reason why that oleander was in that sample, we won't be looking for a missing man, we'll be looking for a suspect."

"There has to be a logical explanation." Meg took a step back to find Jack right behind her as her back met his chest. His hand came to rest on her hip, the warmth of his touch reassuring.

"Meg ..." Riley's voice was gentle. "I don't want to believe there's been a murder in my town any more than you do. I think we've had enough excitement to last us a lifetime, but I have to look at the evidence. And right now, that evidence is pretty damning. Do you have any idea where Nobby is or when he'll be back?"

"No. I wish I did." Meg shook her head, horror mixing with disquiet. "Riley, you can't believe Nobby would do something like that. He's family."

Riley smiled. "No one knows more about what family feuds lead to than the Sullivans and the Morgans. Look how many years it took us to make peace with each other. Were you aware of any trouble between Mary and Nobby?"

Aunty Phyllis scoffed. "What? Those two lovebirds? I'd bet my last cigar the only thing they ever argued over was money."

Interest sparked in Riley's eyes as his gaze flicked to Aunty Phyllis and back to Meg again. "Was there an argument over money?"

Meg sighed. "The only argument was that Granny wouldn't *take* any money from Nobby to cover the running costs of the museum. He wanted to give it to her, as much as he could afford, but she refused it. Granny wanted that grant and the recognition of the Royal Australian Historical Society for the museum, so it could be listed on their registry."

"Doesn't sound like much of a motive for murder, Senior Sergeant Morgan." Jack's hand came to rest on Meg's shoulder.

Riley's gaze narrowed at the movement. "Looks like you've settled in comfortably, Mr Hughes. I hope we won't have any trouble with the press while you're here. We're a small town with limited policing staff. I'd hate for you to attract hordes of unwanted attention."

"You'll get no trouble from me or anyone else associated with me." Jack stiffened against Meg's back, his words coming through clenched teeth.

"Good. Because as much as I don't pay attention to falsified viral online videos, I wouldn't want to add irate politician fathers and their out-of-control daughters to my workload." Riley turned to leave. "If you remember anything, Meg, please come and see me."

"I will, I promise."

Aunty Phyl closed the door behind the senior

sergeant's back. "Oleander. Told you there was someone trying to poison us in this town."

"Aunty Phyl, you can't believe that Nobby had anything to do with it." Horror curled through Meg at the thought of it. Nobby was a life-giver not a life-taker.

"Not saying it was Nobby. But look at that mess with the rustlers last month. Livestock stolen, the Morgans' barn set alight ... no one ever thought we'd see criminals like that living under our noses either. How wrong could we be?"

Jack cleared his throat. "Ladies, let's not jump to conclusions here. Look, when the news gets out about the results, people will talk. The community will be expecting me to ask questions, so maybe I can ask a few discreet ones to see if we can find some answers."

"We need to find bloody Nobby, that's what we need to do. You've got to do something, Meg." Aunty Phyl's voice wobbled.

Meg sighed. Riley's findings would only tear the Band Aid off wounds that hadn't had a chance to heal. "I know, Aunty Phyl. I've been thinking about what to do. It's karaoke night at the Riverside Pub tonight. Almost everyone turns up for that. Jack, you'll have plenty of chances to talk to the locals there. I'll have another dig around in Granny's things, maybe pop over to the garage and see if I can find anything over there that might tell us where Nobby was headed."

"Great idea. I'll head back to the pub and have a

chat with Dan and Alice." Jack gave Meg's shoulder a squeeze. "We'll work it out, ladies."

She took comfort from his touch and his promise. Reporters had a way of asking questions, finding things out. And if Granny Mary had had a good feeling about Jack, then Meg had to trust her intuition. All their questions would be answered as soon as they found Nobby.

CHAPTER SIX

*P*eople drifted into the pub as the karaoke crowd slowly gathered. Jack had spent the afternoon helping Dan set up the stage and equipment while he'd had long chats with Alice's grandad, Charlie, Old Man Jake and any of the patrons who'd drifted in and out. His subtle questions had only confirmed what Meg had said. Nobby Wilkie wouldn't hurt a fly.

He shoved his hands into his pockets after plugging in the speakers. "This is a serious set up."

Dan grinned. "We take our karaoke very seriously. Beer?"

"I thought you'd never ask." Jack swallowed around the dryness in his throat as he spotted Meg and Phyllis walking in. That kiss he and Meg had shared had been burned into his mind and stuck on replay. He wasn't sure he could look Phyllis in the eye ever again.

Dan nodded in their direction, his voice low as he asked, "How's Meg doing? The grapevine will run hot as the rumours start flowing about the results of the tests."

"The toxicology report came as a shock." The light in her eyes had died as she'd withdrawn into her shell. Even now, her face wore a haunted look as she accepted a glass of wine from Alice.

Jack wanted to turn back the clock to that moment when he'd kissed her, when she'd been soft and warm and safe in his arms.

Bloody hell, what was wrong with him? There had to be something strange in the water to make him feel this way about her. He'd never felt like he'd wanted to protect Kelsey. And Meg wasn't the kind of girl who'd want to be protected either.

"Nobby's not a murderer, that's for sure. But he is forgetful sometimes, so it could have been a mistake. I guess we'll have to wait to find out." Dan led the way to the bar, changing the subject. "Hi Meg, Phyl. We'll be serving Mary's brew tonight now that the stock has been given the all clear for contamination. Would you like the honour of the first pull, Meg? Jack's worked up a bit of a thirst."

A glimmer of a smile touched her lips as Meg slipped behind the bar. "Who wants one?"

"I'll have a whiskey later." Phyllis waved a no with her hand.

Alice patted her belly. "I'm on apple juice, thanks."

Dan wrapped his wife in a hug and kissed her forehead. "Apple juice for two, maybe four."

"It's not twins, Daniel." Alice poked a finger in his chest.

"We don't know that for sure yet," Dan answered, his gaze lovingly roaming Alice's face.

Jack wondered why he didn't find their actions lame. He'd never been one for romance and public displays of affection. Yet Dan and Alice made him smile. He turned his attention back to Meg and caught the look of envy that flashed across her features.

Did Alice have what Meg wanted? He pushed the thought away. What did it matter? He was here to cover a story, so best he keep it professional. And to do that, he had to stop replaying that kiss in his head.

Meg grabbed frosted glasses from the fridge and held one under a beer tap. "This is Mary's own special brew. It's a favourite with the townspeople."

Jack watched the golden brew flow into the tipped glass, his mouth watering as the foam head gathered on top, rich and tantalising.

He took the glass she offered, his fingers touching hers. He allowed his hand to linger, enjoying the sensation of her skin against his and the spark that zinged between them.

Her green-blue gaze touched his. Her smile blossomed, lit up the space between them and made his heart flutter. She slipped her fingers from under his and drew her own brew from the tap.

"Cheers," she said, clinking her glass against his.

"Cheers." Jack sipped. Mary's brew was unlike any other he'd enjoyed. Smooth, it eased down his throat, cooled his thirst and warmed his stomach. Full-bodied richness wrapped around his tongue, and he closed his eyes to appreciate the flavour. "Now that's what I call a beer."

Meg chuckled, a sound that shot right down his spine and brought pleasure rocketing through him. What on earth was he thinking? He turned his attention back to the business at hand. "So, what's so special about Mary's brew?"

"Mary's own brand of magic." She leaned forward on the bar counter toward him to share Mary's most important ingredient. "The final step in the brewing process is to run the beer through a filter made from moonstone pebbles Mary imported from Canada during the Vietnam War. You see, moonstones offer protection to those on land and sea, so Mary thought it fitting to filter the beer through the stones. By drinking the brew, she said it would protect you from the inside out and bring peace to the world one beer at a time."

The cynic reared its head. "Well that didn't work did it? There's still far too much death and destruction in the world."

"Yes, but we haven't had another World War, have we?"

Her magical smile chased his scepticism back to the hiding place deep within Jack's heart. He closed the door firmly on it and returned her smile. "True. And I'm quite happy to spread the word. This is a great brew."

He took another sip and looked around the pub. Mellowed by the ambience and the magic of Mary's beer, he hopped off the bar stool and wandered over to an old jukebox in one corner.

He put a dollar into the slot and selected the collection marked Dustscapes and Beer Magic. It seemed appropriate. All his favourites were there — James Blundell, Lee Kernaghan, Troy Cassar Daley, Keith Urban and even good old Slim Dusty, God rest his soul.

Jack had never thought about it until now, but for a city guy, he had a country boy's taste in music. As Keith Urban's *The River* flowed around the pub, he felt the tension slip from his shoulders.

He'd resented this assignment initially. He'd hated being forced from the mayhem of street-reporting by some flighty young kid, so desperate for attention from her parents that she'd resorted to fabricating sex videos to sell on internet video channels with him as the star.

The body double she'd conned into it couldn't easily be identified with his arse in the air all the time. It hadn't taken much to convince viewers that Jack Hughes was the star of her schoolgirl fantasies when the camera had cut to his face at the end. Her video editing skills had been brilliant enough to earn her an honest job if she gave up blackmail.

Until then, here he was in Hell drinking a brew made in Heaven and chatting to an outback fairy about moonstone magic and a missing murder suspect. His next stop would be a padded cell.

"How do you think the oleander ended up in Mary's cup?" Jack brought his attention back to the story as he wandered back to the bar. Dan's mum, Maureen, had taken charge while Dan and Alice danced. Phyllis had wandered off to join in a rowdy game of gin rummy at a table in the corner.

"I wish I knew. I'd still rather believe she died of a broken heart." Meg sighed.

He snorted. "No one dies of a broken heart. That's not a medical condition and it doesn't explain the presence of the oleander."

"You're terribly unromantic, Jack." She leaned her elbow on the bar counter and propped her chin in her hand.

Until he'd met Meg, he hadn't been sure he had a heart, and romance had been the last thing on his mind for a long while. "I prefer to be a realist," he replied. "In my job, you have to be. You see too much of the ugly side of life."

"That's a shame. Everyone should carry a little romance in their pocket." With a sigh, she settled onto a bar stool beside him. "Mary had invested everything she could into the museum. It broke her heart to see it destroyed by all the natural and not so natural disasters that have hit our town. She knew she'd never have sufficient funds to restore the museum without the grant. She worked hard doing all sorts of things to raise funds, including brewing this beer for the pub."

Keith Urban faded to white noise as she spoke. Jack leaned against the bar as he listened to the melodic tones of her voice instead. It flowed over him with a calmness that seeped through his skin, relaxing his tense muscles as the real world drifted away.

"That day, she sat in her rocking chair, sipping her tea with her moonstones in her lap. She put the cup on the floor and then she went to sleep." Meg's voice hitched with sadness. "She never woke up."

Jack looked at Meg's lovely face. Maybe it was Mary's magic or too much beer too quickly. Whatever it was, his heart reached out to hers. "What happened then?"

Meg lifted her head, the sadness back in her eyes. "We tried to wake her up for dinner, but she was gone. Jess Frobisher, our local doctor at the hospital, said her heart had just stopped. It made no sense."

Jack nodded. "So, with the presence of the Melioidosis bacteria in Grady's dam, they thought Mary might have contracted the infection from the water?"

"Correct. Mary had never had a problem with her heart, or her blood pressure, or anything else. She'd been fit and healthy until she got the 'flu, but she was mentally worn out and tired from the years of struggle. Yet still she wouldn't give up. She kept trying for that grant, worked hard to make ends meet, kept going regardless."

"Do you think Nobby could have slipped something into her drink?" A small part of his conscience shuddered at the question, especially when a deep frown furrowed Meg's brow.

"What motive would he have? He loved Mary, long before she married Carrick. Back then, he was a stockman and very good with horses. He had a solid reputation for being a healer. And there was plenty of proof around that his natural methods worked on the farm animals."

"How did he end up working in a garage if his healing skills were in such high demand?"

"After a fall from his horse in the eighties, a badly broken pelvis stopped him from riding as much as he used to. He opened the garage to tinker with cars and machinery." Meg took a sip of her beer. "Nobby made a decent living. He helped Alice out at the animal sanctuary on weekends to earn a little extra. Mary wouldn't take any money from him, so he'd drop a few notes into the donation box when she wasn't looking."

"Why didn't they marry?"

"To Mary and Nobby, a marriage certificate was just a piece of paper. Nobby had nothing to gain from Granny's death. In her will, she left it all to me. The property isn't worth much in the current market, and the museum isn't earning anything aside from the odd visitor or kind donations."

"If he worked at the animal sanctuary, would he have used oleander on any of the animals there? Maybe to put them down? Could he have brought some home with him?"

"Jack! No." The desperation in her tone whacked him hard in the chest. "If there were any animals so ill that they needed to be put down, Nobby would let Alice know to take them to the vet." Her fingers grew white around the glass as she gripped it tight.

"Meg, these are all questions the cops are going to ask. What about Carrick?"

He lifted the glass from her grip and placed it on the bar counter then took her hands in his. He felt the tug of resistance and loosened his hold, leaving her free to pull away if she wanted. But she didn't.

Jack decided he liked the feel of her hands in his, and that thought in itself was dangerous. He was breaking too many of his own rules after only a handful of hours in town.

"Carrick didn't know an oleander tree from a rose bush. Granny told us many stories of his black thumb. Besides, no one has seen or heard from Carrick since he left town. We don't even know if he's still alive."

"Would anyone recognise him if he dropped in?"

Meg shrugged. "I'm sure Aunty Phyl would. Most of the families have been around since the birth of the town, so I'd say the older generations would remember him. But Carrick wouldn't have motive either. Granny

Mary said their split was amicable. No hard feelings on either side."

"Did he know she was pregnant?"

Meg shook her head. "No."

"So, it's possible he might think there's an inheritance in it for him?"

"Possible, but in reality, no. The last time Mary ever heard from Carrick was when their divorce came through. He gave her everything he had left to give in the final settlement. Took nothing for himself except the clothes and a few personal items he'd walked away with. It's not likely news of her death will have made it to Sydney. That will change, of course, when the program goes to air."

Jack felt Meg's shiver trickle through her fingers into his. "Do you think the coverage will flush him out?"

"I never thought about Carrick when I approached the station about airing the story. It's not the way I wanted him to find out about Mary. Or my mother and I."

"Did you try to contact him?"

"Aunty Phyl tried to track him down to let him know Mary had passed, but she couldn't find any trace of him. The lawyers they used in the divorce are long gone, so that too was a dead end." Meg's hands fell away from his as she picked up her glass and sipped.

Jack flattened his palms against his thighs to hold

onto the feel of her a little longer. "So the only way we might find some answers is if we find Nobby."

"I need to find him before the cops go looking for him. He didn't do anything wrong. In my heart, I know that without a doubt."

"Then let me help." Even as the words left his lips, Jack wondered at what point since arriving in town had aliens taken over his mind. Search and rescue had never been part of the plan. The plan had been to get the story and get the hell out of town. Yet here he was, a slave to the plea in Meg's eyes.

"For me or for the story, Jack?"

The punch in her words took his breath away. He paused to think, but not for long. "For you, Meg." Because Meg Moonie was his story. She was the thread that secured the fabric of the story he would present to the nation. "Did Nobby take anything with him when he left?"

"The moonstone ring he gave Granny Mary on the day of their commitment ceremony. With it, he promised to love her forever, in life and after-life. They would be joined forever, would never have to live without each other."

A touch of ice filtered into his blood. "That's kinda sweet." It also sounded awfully like a suicide pact. "Where would you start looking for him?"

"Alice has kept a look out for him locally. His ute hasn't been spotted on any of the park CCTV cameras at his usual spots." She thought about it for a few seconds. "I read in Granny's diary that they used to camp out near Wollomombi Falls when they were younger. The falls are located about a three-hour drive from here in the Oxley Wild Rivers National Park."

Jack shifted on his seat. Three hours-plus in a car and a few nights alone with Meg. Could he risk taking off into the bush alone with a beautiful woman? Uncertainty coiled through him. With that damn video still out there and his innocence yet to be proven, he'd be at risk of muddying Meg's reputation. His reputation had been muddied enough by it, leaving a sour taste on his tongue. It was his word against the daughter of a high profile politician and the odds were stacked against him.

"How long would we need to be away?"

Meg shrugged. "At least a couple of nights."

He had the time. The station was in no rush for the story and the longer he stayed out of town, the faster the hype over the viral video would die down and the better it would be for him. "Is there anyone you trust who we could take with us to help look for him?"

"Not unless we engage SES volunteers, and that would spark a manhunt. I don't want Nobby running scared. I'm worried about him. I was even before Riley came over with that report."

Jack's heart softened a little more at her concern. "Then we'll go and find him. Does he have a radio or a satellite phone with him?"

"He has a two-way radio in his ute, but we haven't

been able to talk him into buying a satellite phone yet. He says they're too expensive. His mobile phone battery would be flat by now unless he's been plugging it into his car charger. And reception is limited when you get that far into the bush. His phone goes straight to message bank when I try to ring."

Unease shivered along Jack's nerve-ends. He didn't like the sound of any of it. He leaned a little closer to Meg. "When do you want to leave?"

"How do I know I can trust you, Jack?" Her face was inches from his.

Hadn't he just asked himself the same question? "Down in the cellar you said Mary chose me. She wouldn't have wanted me here if she didn't have some feelings of trust. I'm happy to take someone else along."

"Take someone else along where?" A cheerful, round, bearded face popped up between them, the owner crouched over with big hands resting on a pair of khaki shorts. "Hello, Jack. What a surprise to see you chatting up the prettiest girl in the room." He held out his hand to Meg. "Hi, I'm Bennie. Jack's one-man camera crew."

Jack didn't try to hide his groan as he shifted a little away. "Perfect timing as always, *Benjamin*." He struggled to keep the sarcasm from his tone. "This is Meg Moonie, Mary's granddaughter. We were just talking about going on a camping trip."

A shudder passed over Bennie's shoulders. "Ugh,

you mean like in places with mosquitoes and snakes and creepy crawlies and stuff?"

Meg laughed. "It's the 'stuff' you need to be afraid of. We do come across the occasional drop bear. Nice to meet you, Bennie."

"Ah, the mythical *thylarctos plummetus*. Eater of eucalyptus leaves, aka the really harmless and cuddly koala." He held onto her hand for longer than Jack felt comfortable with. "Pleasure's all mine."

"Pull up a chair, Bennie." Like on the other side of the room. Jack scowled.

Bennie took a look at Jack's face. "Woah! Okay then. Back up, *ke-mo sah-bee*." He pulled up another bar chair and scooted closer to Meg with a taunting grin on his face.

Jack ground his teeth to stop his tongue from lashing out. Bloody hell, he didn't even know what he was so irritated about. It wasn't like he was jealous or anything. Green monsters had no place in his life. "So, we're taking a camping trip out to the Wollomombi Falls."

Bennie frowned and pointed to his chest. "Jack, does this look like a body that likes to go crawling around in tight spaces and hiking over steep trails? The memo said strictly town coverage."

"Perfect. You can stay here and get some good footage of the town and the people. See you in a couple of days."

"Am I allowed to at least check into my room first?" Bennie winked at Meg.

Jack tried not to let rip the roar that built in his throat. What the hell was wrong with him? Bennie was as harmless as a pet goldfish. "Sure. Go see Alice. The redhead dancing with the bartender. He's the guy with the Riverside Pub apron around his waist."

"Thanks, Jack." He slapped his hands on his thighs and slipped off the bar chair. "See you later." With a salute to Jack and a wink for Meg, he disappeared in the direction of the makeshift dance floor.

"He's nice." Meg smiled at Jack, setting his blood pumping again.

"He's a good cameraman and a decent bloke," Jack conceded. "When would you like to head out? The sooner the better, I'd think, if your senior sergeant is investigating those test results."

"Is tomorrow morning too soon?"

"If you're okay to leave the museum for a couple of days, no problem. Now that Bennie is here, I can get him started on the filming. He knows what to do without direction from me." A trickle of excitement edged into his blood. Footwork and investigation was what he did best.

"I'll let Alice know we're heading out in the morning to start a search. She'll distract Riley from taking any action for a few days."

The spark of hope in her eyes warmed his heart. Jack had never wanted to help someone more than he wanted to help Meg. His biggest challenge would be to protect her reputation. "So it looks like just the two of us." He hoped she really was okay with that.

Her smile, full of trust, delivered the answer he wanted. "Looks that way. Oh, hi, Aunty Phyl."

"Looks like what?" She eyed Jack so sternly he swore he could feel his balls shrivel a little.

"Jack and I are going to see if we can find Nobby."

"Oh really? You think?" Aunty Phyllis eyed him shrewdly before drawing Meg away toward the stage. "I think not. Excuse us. We need to have a word about that and then we've got karaoke business to attend to."

The last he saw of Meg until closing time was her belting out Creedence Clearwater Revival's *Proud Mary*, anchored firmly at her aunt's side.

CHAPTER SEVEN

*M*eg tucked the last of her supplies into her backpack as Aunty Phyl leaned against the door frame to her bedroom.

"I don't like this at all, missy. You don't know the guy from a rat's arse, yet you want to take off into the bush with him. A man who is under suspicion of leading an under-aged girl astray."

"Phyl, you know as well as I do that viral video is rubbish." She tossed in a jumper and tied the straps.

"Didn't say he was guilty, I said he'd been accused. Why can't you take Alice? She's a local ranger."

"Alice is in the middle of a handover of the wildlife rescue to the new guy. She's got enough on her hands."

"Well, I'd be happier if you were taking a chaperone, that's all I'm saying."

Meg turned to hug her aunt hard. "I'll be fine, Phyl. I'm a big girl now."

Phyl hugged her back, holding on a little longer. "You weren't too big to cry rivers when that bastard, Logan, screwed you over. I don't want to see you like that over any man again. Especially not one like Jack Hughes."

Meg wriggled out of her aunt's hug. "We're going looking for Nobby, not getting away for a dirty weekend." Her heart shouldn't beat faster at the thought of being alone under the stars, in the bush, with Jack. With only the protection of a swag between them. "And what exactly is wrong with Jack?"

Phyl ticked off his sins on her fingers. "He's a reporter, a philanderer, a charmer and far too handsome for his own good. Exactly like Logan on all accounts."

A stab of pain tightened Meg's chest. Phyl was right. Lucky Meg had no interest in Jack other than the story he would take to Australia's television screens and the visitors she hoped it would bring to town.

The old brass bell rang out at the front door. "That'll be him now. Let him in, Phyl, and please be nice. I promise you'll have nothing to worry about."

Phyl snorted as she left the room and headed down the hallway to the door. Meg tugged on her boots, tied the laces and hitched up her backpack as Jack's baritone drifted down the hallway.

"Phyllis, you're looking lovely today. Is that a new dress?"

"Charm doesn't flatter me, boy-o. You just take good care of my girl out there."

"I can do that. But I still think that shade of red suits you. Matches your lipstick."

"Cut the crap, Jack." The front door slammed. "But since I don't get compliments often, I'll take that one."

Jack's laugh ran all along the walls and straight up Meg's spine in a pleasant shiver. Phyl had it right on all accounts, and no way would she fall for another charming, roving reporter. No matter how sexy his voice was or what his presence did to her heart rate. Blowing out on a sigh, she stepped into the hallway and walked toward the front door.

Her breath hitched in her throat as she saw Jack. The man did sinful things to denim. The material clung to solid calves and thighs, hugged his hips and had worn to a faded shade of blue in all the areas she shouldn't be looking at.

Heat spread up from her neck into her cheeks as her eyes roamed upward from his scuffed hiking boots, over the snug fit of a dark green T-shirt — that outlined tight washboard abs and strong biceps — to shoulders that looked extra-wide today. Her tongue cleaved to the roof of her mouth, dry and speechless. Hooley dooley, Jack should be banned from ever covering up with business shirts.

Alarm bells rang in her mind. She'd be alone in the bush with all of that. For three days. Minimum.

"Megan?"

She caught Aunty Phyl's use of her full name and the warning look delivered from over her ever-present reading glasses. Forcing her tongue to move, she greeted him, "Hi, Jack."

"Morning, Meg." His soft smile stirred a flutter in her tummy. "Ready to go?"

She nodded, catching Aunty Phyl's eye-roll in her peripheral vision.

"We're taking Bennie's four-wheel-drive SUV. He insisted. The rear seats have been removed so we can sleep in the back if we need to." Jack shifted on his feet.

"Safer than Mary's old ute." Phyl took Meg by the shoulders and pressed a kiss to her forehead. "You take care out there, okay? And bring that old bugger home in one piece."

"We'll do our best."

"As long as you don't do anything else." Her warning look encompassed them both.

The tips of Jack's ears turned red as he opened the front door. "No harm will come to Meg on my watch, Phyllis. Although, I think she's perfectly capable of defending herself. Shall we go?"

"Good idea." Meg returned her aunt's warning look. "I'll be in touch before we lose signal."

"I've got a satellite phone too," Jack reassured Aunty Phyl. "Had to have one for some of the places I've been to."

"Good. Use it. Get Meg to text me the number."

Phyl ushered them out the door. "Drive carefully, Hughes. These aren't city streets."

Jack gave her a cheeky salute as he walked out to the car. Opening the back door, he turned to help Meg with her backpack. Stepping in behind her, he reached for the straps, his fingers brushing her shoulders.

Meg drew in a breath as pleasant tingles rippled through her blood, feeding the doubt that perhaps her aunt was right. Perhaps she shouldn't be alone with Jack.

The weight of the pack slipped from her shoulders and landed with a solid thunk next to his in the rear of the car.

"Maureen packed us some food for the road, and Dan filled up an esky with enough bottled water to supply everyone along the way. He gave strict instructions to bring back the empty bottles for recycling. Oh, and Alice packed some dry rations we can carry with us." The bemusement in Jack's voice filtered through her doubt.

"Alice doesn't take any chances. She's a seasoned bushwalker. Looks like you've made some friends."

His arm brushed against hers as he moved to the passenger side of the vehicle and tiny pulses of pleasure made muscles clench where they had no business tightening. No doubt at all, Jack was slowly sneaking under her skin with his sexy smiles and all-round likeability.

He held open the door. "Bennie's got this thing jacked extra high, so watch your step."

"No problem." Meg put out a hand toward the grab handle to hoist herself up into the seat, only to find it too high out of reach, even on tiptoe.

"Short stuff," Jack teased and patted his shoulders. "Put your hands here."

She braced her hands in the space his had vacated and felt him grip her waist. Seconds later, she sat in the seat looking down into laughing eyes, her hands still glued to his T-shirt, his fingers fanned against her back and her heart racing at a million miles an hour.

The laughter died in Jack's eyes, his hands slipping from around her waist to ball into fists beside her on the seat. His touch barely skimmed her thighs, yet she could feel the heat through her khaki hiking pants. And Jack was in no hurry to move.

Desire flared in his hazel-green eyes, his lips parted and his face inched toward hers. Some invisible strand of magic wound its way around them, shutting out the rest of the world, drawing them closer until she could feel his breath on her lips.

"Jack ..."

Behind them a car engine purred to a stop and a police siren blipped twice. Jack stepped back as Riley Morgan climbed out to lean with one arm on the door and the other on the roof of the police vehicle, his hat in hand.

"Hey, Jack. Meg. Going somewhere interesting?"

"I'm taking Jack camping. Wouldn't want him to leave Bindarra Creek without having the full outback experience." Meg's heart raced for a different reason now that Jack wasn't in her space. If Riley tried to stop them and launch an official search instead, Nobby might run and never be found.

"Right," drawled Riley. "Of course. Well, if you happen to come across Nobby on your trip, tell him I said hi and that I would like a friendly word with him?" The look he gave her spoke volumes. "If you're not back in three days, I'll send out a search party. I don't want to have to explain to Channel Eight how we lost their lead correspondent in the bush."

"Won't happen, Riley. Promise." Mentally, Meg crossed her fingers.

"Make sure it doesn't. See you later. Watch out for snakes." His steady gaze fell on Jack and for a few seconds, the two men eyed each other up, quiet evaluation and assessment passing between them.

"We'll be careful." Jack offered Riley a reassuring nod.

"Good. You do that, Hughes." He slapped his police hat back on his head. "Three days, Meg."

"Thanks, Riley." Relief settled the nerves fluttering in her tummy as he got back in the car and drove away.

"He knows." Jack looked up at Meg.

"Of course he does. Riley Morgan is no one's fool." Meg turned in the seat to slide her legs inside the cab of the SUV and tugged down the seatbelt to secure it in the latch.

"What if he sends a team out anyway?"

Meg shrugged. "He won't."

"How can you be so sure?"

She looked at him, her thoughts coming back to that almost-kiss. If Riley hadn't come along when he had, she'd have kissed Jack twice in as many days.

She couldn't afford any more lapses in judgement. This roving reporter wouldn't be hanging around town once his assignment was done, and she wasn't one to have meaningless flings. No matter how amazing his kisses tasted. "Because Riley Morgan is a man I know I can trust."

Jack closed Meg's door and walked around the front of the four-wheel-drive, the stab from her comment making his ribs ache. Of course she wouldn't trust him when he'd come on to her twice already. And for the second time since arriving, he'd found himself face-to-face with a little green monster. This time in the shape of a cop.

The cheeky devil in his mind taunted him with the fact that Meg had enjoyed that first kiss as much as he had. A second kiss would have been just as sweet, but perhaps Senior Sergeant Morgan's timing had been perfect with that reminder of the reason they were taking this trip. He almost wished he didn't have a story to cover, but then he'd have no reason to be here at all.

A rush of warmth surprised him. He'd thought he'd hate Bindarra Creek, resent being there. Yet he'd begun to enjoy his chats with Dan at the bar, Grandad Charlie's 'dad' jokes and Old Man Jake's insistence Jack call him OMJ so there was no confusion between their names.

Still, there was plenty of time for the novelty to wear off and for his feet to start itching to be on the move again. He wasn't sure why that thought didn't sit well in his mind.

Climbing in beside Meg, he shut the door. "I picked up some takeaway coffee on my way. That stuff from the Cyprus Café is addictive. Thalia twisted my arm into buying some baklava too. I swear it's the best I've ever tasted."

Meg smiled. "She's good, our Thalia. Now, there's another layer for your story. The fire captain, Kel Jones, will tell you all about our resident arsonists. They've caused a lot of damage around town. Some were school kids but then there was one of the council workers who was disgruntled enough to set fire to the council offices."

"Unhappy employee?" Jack started the engine. The more he heard, the more he wondered how this town still existed. They'd had more than their share of hardship.

"Back in August last year, a lot of people lost their

jobs through retrenchment. Mostly those nearing retirement age. Some didn't take it so well. Kel's dad was one of them. But one guy completely lost the plot. He'd served the council for over thirty years."

Jack steered away from the kerb and headed out of town. "Tough times."

"Those who care have stayed to keep fighting. That's the essence of this town. The fires caused a lot of damage, but buildings can be restored. We've got to keep that hope and determination alive."

Jack had seen many things in his travels that had inspired him to donate to causes, but he'd never been stirred to the point that the residents of this small town had. Here, it was all or nothing. Everything and anything.

He'd heard Dan's story of how he'd rescued and renovated the Riverside Pub, and Alice's story of how her wildlife sanctuary came to be. And there were so many more stories out there from people he hadn't had a chance to speak to yet.

Fig Tree Lodge with its resident ghost and history that went back to the first stone laid in the town. Craigellachie and the McGregors who'd introduced the first breeding pair of Highland cattle to the state. The legendary first Mrs McGregor who'd brewed her own whisky in Bindarra Creek's first still, and the ladies of the CWA who played such an important role in keeping the town alive with festivals, fetes and carnivals. And most of all, the community spirit that kept the town alive. Where did anyone find that in the anonymity of city life?

Meg reached for her coffee, her fingers brushing his as he reached over at the same time. Jack slanted a quick look toward her, the touch of her hand sending white-hot need shooting through his veins.

Meg Moonie was like a drug he couldn't get enough of. A dangerous, addictive drug he'd find it difficult to wean himself from when he got his real job back. The thought scared him more than Tamryn Hollister's viral video and seeing an arse that didn't belong to him connected with his face, soiling his reputation.

Yet, still, he wanted to pull the damn car over and kiss her like he'd wanted to kiss her before the cop showed up with a warning in his eyes. That burning need, in turn, made him wonder how much Riley Morgan meant to her. How close were they? And why hadn't she been snapped up by any of the single men in town?

He slid her another glance. Meg was beautiful, kissable, intelligent, strong, gutsy ... and if he didn't keep his eyes on the road and his mind on the job, he'd be inclined to test out number two on her list of attributes again.

Not a good thought when their three-day side trip still had seventy-one hours, fifty-five minutes and thirty-seven seconds to go. He'd been insane to suggest coming along with her, but his conscience hadn't been able to let her go alone.

It had nothing to do with his burgeoning attraction to her. Attraction he could put down to testosterone and pheromones. He was a healthy, red-blooded male and Meg was an incredibly beautiful woman, inside and out.

And when he left town, she would be an incredibly beautiful memory to take with him on the next adventure to the Badlands. Unless he could convince her to travel with him.

The thought blindsided him harder than his need to kiss her. He'd never once thought about asking Kelsey to travel with him. They'd gone their separate ways, carried out their assignments and travels, and caught up with each other whenever their paths crossed. Then they'd got engaged because it seemed like the right thing to do after being together for three years. There'd never been talk of a wedding.

Had he missed something? Is that why Kelsey had gone off her nut and dragged a carving knife across Betty's fender? Jack frowned. No, her anger had been at the fact her good name and reputation had also been dragged into the scandal by a mischief-making young girl desperate for her parents' attention.

A sigh slipped from Jack's lips as the navigation system told him to take the A15 at the third exit.

"That's a big sigh, Jack. I thought you'd be a little more talkative."

"Didn't want to miss the turn off." He pushed his rambling thoughts back into their box. "So, tell me more about where we're going."

Meg turned a little in her seat to look at him. "After the rains, the Wollomombi Falls cascade two hundred and twenty metres onto the valley floor with a spectacular view from the rim. It's been a bit dry since the storm and flash flood back in July, so I'm not sure how much fall there'll be. The park has basic barbecue facilities, toilets and a handful of small camping grounds."

"Which one do you think Nobby will be at?" Jack cast her a glance, hearing concern sneaking into her voice.

Meg ran a hand up her arm, rubbing at her skin. "Wollomombi has two walking tracks. The Chandler track is the most challenging, and Nobby loves a challenge. He'd try to get to the river to be near water, even though that part of the track has been closed due to erosion. He'd find a safe path to get there and head toward Long Point."

"Why Long Point?" Jack had no idea where or what Long Point was, but he was about to find out. The hard way. He'd done some research and realised it would be tough terrain for someone fit and healthy to navigate. He had no idea what kind of shape Nobby was in.

"Brumbies. Nobby has always been drawn to them."

Jack shivered. Horses weren't his thing. Not even steel ones, although he'd ridden a few of those in his time. Wild horses were better viewed on the screen, in a movie or a *National Geographic* documentary. "What if he isn't at Wollomombi?"

Meg reached into the leg pocket in her hiking pants and pulled out a little black book. Flicking through it, she stopped at a page. "In her diary, Mary talks about a place near the Chandler River where she and Nobby camped. It's there they promised themselves to each other, so I'm guessing that's where he'd head to say goodbye. But there are no specific landmarks or coordinates to go by."

"Bennie has something in the back that might help."

Interest sparked in her voice. "Yes?"

Jack grinned. "A drone. Long range, top-deck geek quality with spare long-life batteries."

"Sounds expensive. What if it gets lost or damaged? It's rocky, tree-filled terrain in the gorge."

"It's insured, but I've promised him I'll replace it if something happens to it that insurance won't cover. We often use it to record footage for program coverage. He'd planned to fly it into Bindarra Creek as a bird's eye intro to the town."

A soft smile spread her lips, wrapping Jack in its magic. "We'd have to put in an application for permission to fly a drone in the park. I can do that online from my phone. It might help us spot Nobby's camp site."

"That's what I'm hoping for." Because being alone in the wild too long with Meg would test every ounce of his resistance not to kiss her again. Her mouth was a drug he could too easily get hooked on, and Meg wasn't a love-em-and-leave-em kinda girl.

CHAPTER EIGHT

*T*hree hours alone in a car with Jack. Meg found herself liking him more with every passing stretch of road. Once he started talking, she became captivated by his interesting stories. This man was a far cry from the deviant portrayed on the news by Tamryn Hollister and her father. Mary had chosen him well.

His deep, sexy baritone flowed easily between them. Meg could happily listen to him talk all day, except that by the end of it, she'd be high-voltage wired by the tug of attraction he stirred in her.

As it was, her mouth was dry from the sight of his hands on the wheel and the strength in his arms as he navigated bends and overtaking lanes. But it wasn't only his sex appeal that drew her into a state of relaxed trust.

The more he spoke, the more she got to see the

softer side of the hardened world feature correspondent.

He liked dogs, although he'd never had one himself, and wasn't a big fan of cats unless they were wild and African.

After doing a story on rhino poaching, he'd made a large donation to a South African rescue facility and anti-poaching movement to save the white rhino.

He sponsored five children in poor countries across the world and had visited them all, knew their names, and tracked their progress every year. A man who did all that couldn't be all that bad, could he? But then, inside every saint was a sinner, right?

Yet, he'd told her the stories with a heartfelt smile on his face and genuine pride in his voice. He hadn't done these things for recognition; he'd done them because he really cared about the outcomes for the people he'd helped. How could a girl not like an all-round nice guy like Jack?

Everything he'd told her proved he was different from Logan. With her rose-coloured glasses off, she'd acknowledged that Logan had more than earned the insensitive, narcissistic arse-hat title bestowed on him by Aunty Phyl.

If Meg had wised up earlier, she would have seen the clues. But love had truly been blind and she had believed herself to be in love with Logan. Older and wiser, she wouldn't make the mistake again of falling for a man with itchy feet and a silver tongue.

But, oh lordy, Jack's tongue did wonderful things to kisses. His hands on her hips, her arms, her back ... how could she not wish to feel that magic? Without the barrier of clothing and untimely interruptions from well-meaning aunts.

God knows what might have happened if Riley Morgan hadn't come to the museum when he had. She would have climbed Jack like a monkey and done some dirty dancing right there in the middle of Granny Mary's most prized, yet damaged, collections. The memory brought with it a groan that escaped her lips.

Jack looked across at her with a chuckle. "Are you okay over there in the corner?"

Heat filled her cheeks. "Yep, just looking forward to getting out and stretching my legs."

"Not far to go now according to the GPS. The turn off should be somewhere ... here." Jack navigated the sealed road into the park and stopped at the self-registration booth. "Looks pretty deserted."

Disappointment sank like a stone in Meg's tummy. Her hopes had been pinned on finding Nobby quickly. Had she got it wrong? What if all of this was a waste of time, a job she should have left to the SES?

Jack rolled forward toward the camping ground and together they picked the best spot to set up camp. The park looked drier than the last time she'd been there. Green had turned to brown, blending in with the wooden structure that housed the barbecue facilities. The information board still stood strong against the backdrop of the gorge. And the park showed no sign of Nobby's ute.

"I'm sorry, Meg." Jack reached out to touch her arm. "I know you were hoping he would be easy to find. Are there any other campsites nearby?"

"Long Point is about a four-day hike from here along the Chandler River. He may have camped there." She tried hard not to let the crack in her voice slip through, but it did.

"We could drive around there and check."

Meg shook her head, trepidation a solid mass in her throat. She opened the door, climbed out and walked to the edge of the trees. The gorge opened up before her, a mass of green mountains and valleys that faded to greyish blue in the distance. Varieties of gum trees towered on the slopes below, and somewhere down there, the river.

If Jack knew what she was about to do, he'd freak out. Or laugh at her. She wasn't sure which would be the lesser of the two evils, but she did know, with an urgency in her heart, that she needed to find Nobby.

She closed her eyes and tuned in to the sounds of the wild. The call of the eagles, the rustle of the trees and the distant rush of water into the gorge. And as Mary had taught her, she silenced her thoughts to open her mind to nature, searching for sounds that were out of place. An indication of human life among the birds, brumbies, rock wallabies and echidnas.

Meg breathed deep, inhaling the scent of nature,

sorting through the different smells, identifying them one by one. Searching for the signature olfactory tag that would identify Nobby. Science not magic. Nobby's olfactory print smelled like woodsmoke and pine trees, sunshine and rain, all wrapped up in the rusty scent of old metal. She caught a hint of it from below before Jack's print overrode it.

Now Jack ... he was a hotbed of heady scents. A promise of long, hot nights, tangled sheets, a hint of musk in his soap, and the citrusy tang of expensive aftershave. And, oh boy, did she want to taste him.

His warmth filled the space behind her. "We'll find him, Meg. I promise."

"He's here, Jack. I know he is. We just need to figure out where."

"Let's set up a base camp, have something to eat and drink, and then take a walk while we wait for approval to come through to use the drone." There was comfort in the squeeze of his hand on her shoulder.

Meg leaned into his touch, absorbing his strength, trusting his solidarity. He wouldn't have made this trip with her if he didn't truly want to help.

For a while longer, they stood. Taking in the raw and rugged beauty of New England wilderness, and the unforgiving power of nature only the toughest could survive. How strong would Nobby be without his Mary?

For once, Meg was glad she didn't have to do this alone. She'd been the one to stay strong when Aunty

Phyl had fallen apart, incapable of making the necessary funeral arrangements. And when Nobby had retreated into his shell after the burial. Withdrawing from his friends and even the Lawson kids. Unable to do anything but stand on the crumbling verandah and stare in the direction of the cemetery, a silent, broken man.

Then had come the questions, the testing of the water. Another rock piled on top of the problems that plagued their town, just when things had started to look up. And all Meg had wanted to do was fix things the way Mary had wanted so that wherever she was, she could see her dream come true and her legacy live on. So that those around her would smile when they remembered Mary and how much she'd done for the town.

But unless Jack's portrayal of their town's struggle to survive, and the importance of keeping the museum open in a reasonable state, could be recognised by the world outside Bindarra Creek, she had a slim chance of ever winning that restoration grant from the Royal Historical Society.

And if rumours got out that tests had found poison in Mary's tea, Bindarra Creek would rise to fame for all the wrong reasons.

Meg Moonie made Jack feel things he'd never felt

before. Tenderness. Longing. A need to hold her and never let her go. It should have scared him, made him run a mile.

Instead, he wanted to turn her around. Kiss her. Make her promises he'd never made to anyone else. What kind of madness was that?

Reluctantly, he eased away. "The Pajero has a rooftop tent. Would you prefer that to sleeping in the back?"

Common sense hammered the message into his head that it would be better if they didn't share the tent or the back of the car. Waking up next to Meg, all warm and sleepy, and him aroused — not a great idea for a man determined to stay away from women. Especially a woman who'd captured his good sense and didn't deserve to be hurt by what was going down in his life right now.

"There'd be a great view from the top in the tent. The gorge always delivers amazing sunsets and sunrises. And the stars out here will be brighter than any you'll ever see in the city." Meg smiled softly up at him.

"I've seen stars in many places. Some not nearly as peaceful as this. I think these will be spectacular." More because of the company than the setting.

Everything Meg did or saw came coupled with enthusiasm. Except for today. He'd sensed a change in her as she'd stood at the edge of the gorge, a melancholy he wished he could tease away.

They walked back to the car, side by side, arms brushing, fever building. A fever he'd be wise to ignore. But when had risk-taker Jack Hughes ever been wise?

This time.

Jack eyed the rooftop tent inside its hard shell and almost wished Bennie had come along.

For a guy who'd said he didn't like camping, Bennie had all the gear. *Bought it like that. Came as a package deal. Never used it. Not sure a tent like that could handle a big guy like me.* Bennie's grin had said he was lying through his teeth and just not keen on playing third wheel.

Laughter chased the melancholy from Meg's eyes. "What's the matter, city boy? Don't know how to get it up?" Jack cast her an amused look as she gasped. "Oh my God, that came out all wrong. I meant ... I mean ... the tent, Jack." Heat rushed into her cheeks.

"Really? Because that's what I thought you meant. Are you sure that's what you meant, Meg?" He couldn't resist teasing her as warmth glowed in her cheeks. "Because, you know, I'd be quite happy to demonstrate."

She swallowed hard, a giggle sticking in her throat. "Jack ..." Her gaze dropped to his mouth, laughter dying to give way to something hotter as she leaned back onto the car.

Jack leaned in, bracing his weight with his hands flat against the warm metal of the four-wheel-drive, his lips a whisper from hers. "Say no and I walk away."

Her hands crept up his chest to cup his face, her gaze holding his. "Kiss me again, Jack." She drew his face closer, touched her mouth to his.

Whatever control Jack may have had left fled under the tease of her tongue. He gathered her close, fitted her curves neatly to his and kissed her until they were forced to lift their heads to breathe. Then he went back for more because he'd never tasted anything as sweet and heady as Meg.

Moulded against him, her hands were everywhere, leaving tiny shots of electric charge wherever they touched. She'd be in no doubt now as to the answer to her question as he pressed against her and let the car take their weight. He lifted her up until her legs anchored around his waist, her hands clutched the back of his head, and he held a firecracker in his arms.

Jack let go of her mouth to bury his head in her neck. If he didn't stop now, he wouldn't be able to stop at all. Her fingers brushed his hair, his ear, and when her hips shifted against his, he almost came undone.

"Meg," he breathed into her skin.

Need clawed at him in a whole new way. He didn't want to have sex with Meg. He wanted to slow it down and make love to her. Somewhere nice. Not in the middle of a national park in the back of a borrowed Pajero. The realisation had his hands trembling on her body. This wasn't simply a carnal urge he'd be satisfying. Another first for Jack Hughes, and it scared him enough to hesitate.

He lifted his face to hers. "You're beautiful, Meg, but I don't know what we're starting here. I don't know if we should be starting anything."

Her palms skimmed his shoulders, his back, raising his need to a whole new level. "Then hold me. Just hold me," she whispered.

"That I can do."

He carried her over to the picnic table with her arms around his neck, her legs around his waist. Then he sat on the bench with her in his lap and held her tight.

The world around them faded until it existed only of the woman in his arms. Her scent, the silky feel of her skin, and the shape of her against him. Jack closed his eyes and allowed his senses to engage.

He struggled with a newly discovered emotion that lodged in his throat. When had he grown to care about her, this stranger from a small town off the beaten track? A girl so far out of his comfort zone, they were worlds apart.

Her sigh whispered across his ear. "Do you ever grow tired of being strong, Jack?"

Did he? In the wake of the release of that video, he'd wanted to crawl into a hole somewhere and only come out when the hype was over. The reason Bindarra Creek had seemed like the best idea at the time. The fallout could spell the end of his career.

Should he have gone against the advice of his superiors and stayed to fight for his honour, rather than let the station's legal department handle it? No, they were the professionals when it came to dealing with bad publicity. He'd been right to let them do their job.

"I think everyone has their limit of endurance." That was true, wasn't it?

Her arms fell away from his shoulders and cool air came between them as she moved back a little, tipping her face up to his. "How long do I keep fighting to keep Mary's dream alive? What if we do all this and I still don't get that grant?"

"There's no harm in fighting for what you're passionate about. The question is: are you doing it for Mary or for yourself? Is it your dream too, Meg?"

"I've loved the museum for as long as I can remember. I shared Mary's dream to bring it back to life. Everything in those rooms has a story to tell, and I want to safeguard those stories as much as she did. I want people to know how this town came to be, how hard we've worked to save it, to preserve it. If we let the history die, everything generations before us worked hard to build will die too."

"Can you imagine yourself anywhere else in the world other than Bindarra Creek?" He wasn't sure why the answer might tie a knot in his stomach or why it mattered.

She thought a moment, her gaze directed somewhere over his shoulder. "No. This is my home, Jack. This is me."

"Then keep fighting for what you believe in, Meg.

That's why I'm here to cover the story, to help you get that message across." And for the first time since arriving in town, Jack realised he meant it. If it meant that much to her, he'd do everything he could to help her secure that grant.

CHAPTER NINE

*M*eg wriggled off Jack's lap and stood. She'd spent too long in his arms already. Allowed her guard to slip under the pleasure of his kiss. How easy it would be to lean on him, to let someone else take control for once. But after the program went to air, Jack would be gone, and life in Bindarra Creek would carry on. First, they had to find Nobby.

"It's getting late. We should get moving so we can cover some ground before we lose too much light."

Jack moved toward the car. "I'll set up the tent. How far do you plan to go today?"

"Far enough to pick up any trail markers Nobby might have left. If we're in the right spot, we can start out early tomorrow morning, go further, and maybe camp along the river overnight." She didn't want to think about not finding any signs to prove her olfactory senses right.

Jack climbed up on the rear wheel of the car and unhitched the straps securing the lid of the hard shell box that housed the tent. Moving around, he pushed up first one end, then the other, affording Meg a pleasing view of muscles and man.

She and Mary had more than the museum in common. Jack would walk away just like Carrick and Logan had, so best she didn't become too attached to his kisses and the way he'd held her, making her feel whole again.

He brought the ladder down and hooked it to the side of the car. Turning around, he caught her looking and grinned.

Warmth flushed her cheeks. "I'll pack a bag to take along. Water, snacks, a jumper because it gets cooler down in the gorge."

"Great idea." Laughter twinkled in his eyes.

She reached into the back of the Pajero and started rearranging things in her backpack. "Tomorrow, we'll each take our own backpack. We'll have to take swags too."

He leaned up against the rear frame, arms folded, and watched her shuffle things in and out of the backpack. "Do we know where we're going?"

Meg tried hard not to look. She'd always been a sucker for strong arms. "The trail is marked out, but it stops before reaching the river. We'll have to mark out our own track from there so we can find our way back." Her phone pinged and she pulled it out of her pocket to check her email. "We've got approval to use the drone." Relief flooded her. Perhaps the drone would find Nobby quicker than they could on foot, or at least give them a direction to search in.

"The drone is in one backpack, so we'll have to limit supplies to the other."

"I can carry some weight." Meg teased him by showing him her own muscles. "I'm tougher than I look."

"Didn't doubt that for a minute." His gaze intensified as his fingers trailed over her arm. "You've got some good muscles there, Meg."

"Thanks." The word came out on a whisper, his touch stealing her breath.

For a minute, she thought he would kiss her again, but Jack pushed away from the car. "We'll take the drone tomorrow. Should we lock up the car and see what we find without it?"

Meg dropped two bottles of water into her pack and strapped it up. "Sure." She squashed the rise of disappointment. Kissing Jack was fast becoming an addiction. One she couldn't afford to get hooked on because he'd break her heart by leaving, like Logan had. A small town like Bindarra Creek couldn't hold adventurers and thrill-seekers.

Moving away so he could close the doors and lock them, Meg hitched the backpack onto her shoulders.

She wandered over to the start of the walking trail, waiting for him to catch up, thoughts churning in her head.

The Moonie women didn't have a great track record in keeping their men. Meg's mystery father. Carrick. Logan. The man Aunty Phyl let walk away too. All travellers, city people, not locals. All of them only seeing a dying town and none of them willing to stay and save it.

That's why Mary and Nobby had been made for each other. They'd shared their love for each other, and for Bindarra Creek. It made no sense that Nobby would poison Mary's tea. He'd had no motive.

"Ready?" Jack filled the space beside her, dragging her out of her thoughts.

"Checks Lookout is about a third of the way on this trail. We'll get a good view along the gorge to the falls from there. It's a short walk, about a two-hour round trip, but we can start marking out our own trail at the end of it for another three or four kilometres. I think that's as far as we should go today or we won't make it back to camp before dark. Nobby has a bright orange tent, so we might be lucky to spot him as we get closer to the river."

Meg started down the wooden stairs that led to the track with Jack a step or two behind her. Above them, a wedge-tailed eagle surfed the thermals, soaring above the steep cliffs, then swooping down to glide along the narrow gorge.

Not for the first time, Meg wished she had wings to fly. To soar the skies and forget about the burdens for once. What if they didn't find Nobby? What if he never came back? She thought of the kids, their spirit garden, and how much everyone loved Nobby. What if he had murdered Mary?

Her boot slipped a little as her foot touched the track, making her skid unsteadily in the dirt.

Jack's hand shot out to steady her. "Are you okay?"

"I'm fine." He stood too close, his essence of being stealing control of her senses.

She'd always been tough and independent, more so after Logan. So what made Jack so different? His touch settled the roil of uncertainty in her stomach, the clash of thoughts in her mind. Never before had she wanted to climb into someone's skin the way she wanted to with Jack.

Maybe bringing him along on this search for Nobby hadn't been the best of ideas. He distracted her in too many ways, interfered with her senses and focus.

"We should move on." She made the mistake of looking up at him. His eyes burned with a mixture of concern, confusion and desire. Jack was as unsettled by this connection between them as she was.

His hand fell away, leaving tingles where his fingers had been and too many questions in her mind. Live for the moment, give in to the attraction now, and deal with a broken heart later. No one had ever died from a broken heart, but many had lived with regrets.

Whatever happened from today on, she couldn't deny that Jack's presence had shifted something in her universe that would never be the same when he left.

They walked on in silence, the song of the birds and the sounds of the bush echoing around the gorge. Reaching the lookout, Meg stopped and placed her hands on the railing to take in the view around them.

Jack stood beside her, his hands close to hers. "It's a different world down here, isn't it? Like some kind of magical lost and forgotten land."

Meg smiled. "Wait until we get closer to the river. You haven't seen magic until you've watched a herd of wild brumbies run."

"The drone will capture some great footage to add to the segment."

"Yes, it should. I understand why Nobby likes to come out here. It's beautiful." The breeze blew a strand of hair across her cheek.

Jack brushed it back and tucked it behind her ear, leaving heat to follow the trail of his fingers and awareness fizzing through her. "Very beautiful."

She could feel the intensity of his gaze. Meg looked at him, her heart pounding against her rib cage. His eyes were on her face.

Jack moved a little closer. "You look like you belong here, Meg. An outback fairy born out of the wild beauty of the gorge." His fingers traced the shape of her ears, her cheeks, her lips, leaving fire trailing in their wake. "That's what I thought you were the first time I met you."

"I'm very real, Jack."

"I don't doubt that for a minute." His words whispered close to her lips before he closed the distance between them. His kiss this time was light, barely a skim of his mouth on hers before he inched away. "I'm not sure how, but you've got me under some kind of spell."

Doubt crept in, dispelling the magic. Jack Hughes had a reputation with women. Whether the reports were true or not, Aunty Phyllis had warned her about the presence of smoke usually indicating fire. And Jack was pretty damn hot. "I bet you say that to all the girls."

Hurt flashed across his features as he drew back. He replaced it with a tight smile, his eyes on the eagle still dancing on the thermal drifts. Meg wished she could take the words back as she felt his withdrawal, but it was for the best.

"We should move on."

Jack nodded and pushed away from the railing. Silently, he led the way this time, his shoulders tense and his spine stiff.

The irony of Meg's words hit him with a punch to the gut. He had used those words before, but never had he meant them as much as he had just then. And now he wavered between insulted and terrified.

Behind him, Meg's boots crunched against the dirt. She had him tied in knots. His mind, his gut and everything north and south too. He'd never been in this deep or *felt* at this level before.

An uncomfortable silence lay between them as they walked. Jack wished he could unsay the words that had driven the distance between them. Meg Moonie was an unknown entity. She didn't frolic in the realms he was used to. This girl was sweet, innocent and guileless.

He pictured himself walking out of town the way he'd walked in. With the plan to get the story and get out. The twist in his gut said it was too late for that. Meg, the town, the people had already found their way past his barriers.

The trail ended abruptly where the path had been barred and warning signs of erosion spoke of dangerous falls. Meg's arm brushed his as she stepped around him to peer down at where the slope had crumbled.

"There's a service track up the slope to the left we could follow until the ground is more stable."

Jack allowed his gaze to follow the direction in which she pointed. "It's a bit of a climb to get up there."

"Scared, Jack?"

"Terrified." But not of the climb or of the slope.

"Don't worry, I'll hold your hand." She reached for

it, threading her fingers through his. "I'm sorry. I didn't mean to make you angry."

"I'm not angry. Not with you. You're right, Meg. With everything that's happened in these last couple of months, I've had to take a good, long, hard look at myself. And I've realised I don't like what I see." He squeezed her fingers, liking the feel of them against his. "Living life the way I have, I left myself open to be a target to girls like Tamryn Hollister. Being a public figure always comes at a cost. A cost that often means we lose sight of who we really are or who we want to be."

Meg's smile set his heart pounding. "If ever there's a place for you to find yourself, then this is it." Her fingers slipped from around his as she spread her arms wide. "Out here there is only nature and clarity. Fresh air to clear your mind. And exercise to tire your body so you can sleep and wake refreshed. That's what Nobby believes, and why he goes bush every now and then."

"Sounds like good medicine." It was hard to stay angry when her smile brought sunshine to the shade. "Ready to climb that hill?"

"Ready when you are. Race you to the top?"

Jack eyed the incline. "You're kidding, right?"

She took off like a mountain goat, with the confidence of someone who'd negotiated the climb a few times. He shook his head as he followed at a more cautious pace. God only knew what perils lay in the thick undergrowth.

By the time he reached the top, Meg stood leaning against a tree waiting for him, a victoriously cheeky grin on her lips. "Smart arse," he muttered as he reached her.

She held out a bottle of water. "Have a drink. We don't want you dehydrating."

He took the bottle from her, twisted the top off and drank. Whoever said water was tasteless had lied. The cool liquid slid down his throat sweeter than honey. Jack let out a satisfied sigh before handing the bottle back to Meg. "Cheers."

She dropped the bottle into her backpack, tied the straps and hoisted it up onto her shoulders. "If you've got your breath back, we should get moving."

"Want me to carry the backpack for a while?" He knew how damn heavy those things could feel after a while.

"No, thanks. It's a lot lighter than it will be tomorrow when we head out." She started walking and Jack followed. "Another two or three kilometres will give us an idea of a stable trail to follow down to the river tomorrow. If we can't access it from here. We might have to move camp to Long Point and start our search from there."

"Why don't we do that anyway?"

"If Nobby started out from Long Point, he'd be closer to Wollomombi now than he'd be to his starting point. All the trails pretty much lead to the river, and that's where he'll head to be close to water."

"If ever I have to trek through the Amazon rainforest, I'm taking you with me. You think a lot more logically than Bennie does."

Meg's laugh bounced of the trees. "I like Bennie. He's like a big, energetic St Bernard, and they're pretty good tracking dogs, so you'd be just fine with him."

Her reassurance didn't stop him wondering what it would be like to have Meg on his team and have her with him on every assignment. She had drive and determination. The thought grew on him. What if he could convince her that there was a life for her beyond the museum and Bindarra Creek?

But then he'd never belonged anywhere in the same way Meg did. She belonged here in the community and the town she clearly loved so much. She'd be out of place in the cities of the world, every bit the fairy escaped from the outback.

In contrast to the women who had crossed his path over time, Meg was earthy, fresh, grounded. Her natural beauty, inside and out, wrapped itself around a man's heart and held it captive. He'd seen it in Bennie.

A twinge of jealousy twisted a knife under his ribs. Damn Bennie with his puppy dog eyes. He'd all but had to roll the kid's tongue up off the floor and put it back in his mouth when he'd introduced Meg. Jack had never batted an eyelid when Bennie went gaga over Kelsey, so why should he feel so differently about Meg?

They reached a bend in the service track where it ran in the opposite direction of where they wanted to be. Meg stopped walking and surveyed the slope back down into the gorge.

"If you look carefully, you'll see the brumbies have worn a path down to the water."

Jack followed her direction, seeing where the undergrowth had been flattened by the brumbies' hooves. "So we follow in their path?"

Meg nodded. "Yes. I've got some of Nobby's bio-degradable plant ties to mark our trail. We'll tack those on every three minutes until we reach the river."

"And I'm guessing we'll have to mark a re-entry point?"

"We'll make a boy scout of you yet, Jack." She removed a bright orange tie from her pocket and secured it to a branch on a tree. "We'll start out here tomorrow after I've let the local ranger know our starting point and time."

Foreboding tickled his senses. "Why? Do you think we'll get lost?"

"I promised Alice I'd leave a starting point for them to follow if we don't make it back to town within the three days Riley has given us."

"Fair enough." He wondered why being lost in the wilderness didn't bother him so much with Meg by his side. On his other assignments, he'd been itching to get back to the city by the time they were over. That restless energy he normally felt was missing out here. "Does that mean we're heading back to camp?"

Meg checked her watch. "I think that's a good idea. The light goes fast out here. If we leave at dawn tomorrow, we'll make good time down to the river and be able to follow it for a few kilometres before finding a spot to set up camp."

"Great. Let me carry the backpack. Save your shoulders for tomorrow."

Meg eased the pack off her back and handed to him. "Thanks."

Hitching it onto his shoulders, he turned back onto the service track. "Please tell me you're not going to make me slide down that slope we climbed."

Meg grinned. "Nope. This track leads back into the picnic grounds but comes out on the opposite end to where we are. We'll cut back onto the trail at level ground this time."

"You mean to tell me that there was an alternative to the slope all along? You're a cruel woman, Meg Moonie."

"Life wasn't meant to be easy, city boy. Besides, I was testing your endurance with that slope. No point taking you down into the gorge if you can't get back out."

Jack chuckled. "That's the second time you've questioned my endurance today. I thought we'd settled the answer on that one."

Heat flushed Meg's cheeks. "The biggest test of

your endurance is yet to come. I get to stretch out in the tent, while you get to curl up in the back of the Pajero."

She had that one right. He doubted he'd sleep a wink knowing she lay on the roof above him, all warm and sleepy in that tent. He'd be walking that trail tomorrow stiff, sore and ridiculously frustrated. Jack hoped the water in the river would be deep enough and cold enough to cool off in when they reached it.

CHAPTER TEN

*I*n the torchlight, Meg checked her watch. First light would be appearing on the horizon. She'd barely slept. The occasional rock of the Pajero told her Jack had had trouble sleeping too. She'd heard the rear door open sometime in the night and she'd looked out to see Jack sitting on the hood, back against the windscreen, staring at the stars.

For a long minute, she'd thought about joining him out there, but that would be inviting trouble with such a potent attraction between them. No point starting something that would only bring heartache and regret.

Last night, they'd had dinner cooked over the fire pit, talked about Jack's adventures, avoided discussion over the viral video and public break up with his long-time girlfriend, Kelsey McDonnell, and gone their separate ways to bed.

All very grown up and responsible when the devil

inside her had been tempted to invite Jack up into the tent and test that endurance she'd teased him about. Perhaps they both would have slept better.

"Meg," he called to her softly.

She propped herself up on her elbow. "Yeah?"

"Want to come down and watch the sunrise? I've got instant coffee and a sandwich for breakfast."

God bless the man. "I'll be right down."

She wriggled into her track pants and pulled on a hoodie before unzipping the tent flap and shimmying down the ladder. Firm hands gripped her waist and lifted her off the last rung.

Meg turned to find her nose level with his naked chest and her hands automatically reaching for his hips. He smelled like soap, herbs and musk. She inhaled the heady scent for a moment before good sense kicked in. She should step back from temptation. "Put some clothes on, Jack. You'll catch a cold."

His chuckle vibrated off his chest. "I've just had a wash in freezing cold water. I think I've been cryogenically preserved."

He wasn't kidding. The light sprinkling of chest hair that covered his breastbone before arrowing south did nothing to keep two manly nipples warm. Her palms itched to follow the contours of his body to the edge of his track pants and beyond.

"Bathroom's all yours." He'd rigged a privacy screen around the back of the Pajero. "I've warmed the bucket of water up for you."

"You know a lot about camping for a city boy."

His grin almost made her knees collapse. Jack showed her his phone. "Bennie's instructions."

"I owe Bennie a drink at the pub." She realised she was still talking to his chest and looked up at his face. "Thanks, Jack."

"You're welcome." For a minute he looked intensely at her, and Meg's heart pounded. But when a kiss didn't follow and he said, "You've got eight minutes to sunrise," she moved out of his space and around the back of the car.

It would be too easy to be distracted by a man like Jack. Meg dragged a change of clothes out of the back of the car and re-focused on washing, getting dressed and brushing her teeth. Today had to be about finding Nobby.

Determination chased the unease from her mind. When they found him, he'd explain everything. There had to be an innocent explanation, at least from Nobby's end. Nobby was a healer, not a murderer. And Meg couldn't think of anyone in Bindarra Creek or outside of it who would purposely poison Mary.

Meg cleaned up, packed away Jack's makeshift wash facilities, and stowed everything away as the sky began to change colour with the rising sun. She joined him at the rim of the gorge and accepted the cup of coffee he pressed into her hands.

To the east, the sun rose gracefully, bathing the mountains and forests in shifting hues of gold, catching the spray of the falls and casting rainbows across the valleys. A comfortable silence lay between them as they watched the new day begin.

Beside her, Jack sighed. "I've never seen a sunrise as enchanting as that."

"But you've been to so many places all over the world?" Surprise made her look away from the mesmerising view to raise her gaze to his face.

He shrugged. "On location, we never had time to stop and take in the scenery. In the war zones, they got us in and out as quickly as possible. In Africa, we dodged poachers, so most of the reports were done in the middle of the night or long after the sun had risen to reveal the devastation of their spoils."

"You've seen an ugly side of life."

"Too much." Regret coloured his words.

"Yet when you're done here, you'll go back to that life." Her heart ached at the reality of that thought. Why was she always attracted to the ones who walked away? Except this time, it was different. She felt more than just attraction to Jack.

"It's what I do. I go out there, report, hope that what I do will make a difference, maybe change things." He turned away from the view. "It's time to find Nobby. I'll pack away the tent and lock up the car."

"Okay." Meg handed him her empty enamel mug when he held out his hand for it.

She pushed aside the melancholy that had gripped

her chest. Mary had said she'd seen Meg's future and the man in it, but perhaps that man wasn't Jack.

Meg checked for signal on her phone. Still good for now. They'd lose signal once they entered the gorge. "I'll let the ranger know we're heading out."

They'd packed their backpacks the night before, ready to leave at first light. In silence, they worked together to pack up their things. Jack hitched the backpack onto his back, loaded with the drone and the ultra-lightweight double swag.

Meg eyed the swag nervously. Sharing it with Jack would put them in even closer proximity than the rooftop tent would have. Perhaps they'd find Nobby before nightfall and then they wouldn't need to camp out along the river.

"Ready?" Jack came around to help her load her pack. "How does that feel?"

"Good."

His fingers grazed her shoulders as he adjusted the straps, skimmed her waist and hips as he bent to secure the front fastening. Blood fizzed through her veins to colour her cheeks. He straightened, coming up so close she could almost feel the brush of the two-day growth of stubble on his face. Her fingers itched to skim his jaw, to feel the scratch against her skin.

"Don't look at me like that." His words whispered across her lips. "I'm having a hard time trying to be a gentleman right now."

For a mad moment, Meg wanted to tell him to stop

trying. She averted her gaze to somewhere over his shoulder. "I'll lead the way once we reach the track we marked out yesterday."

"Sounds good." He stepped away and cool morning air came between them. Jack dropped the Pajero keys into a side pocket on her pack. "These will be safer in your pack than mine. My side pockets are full of drone parts."

With one last check to make sure the Pajero was secured, they walked in the direction of the service road. Jack kept a good distance between them as they walked, silent in his own space.

Meg focused on tuning into the sounds and smell of nature, sorting through them to catch a hint of Nobby's direction. As they neared the start of the track, unease found its way into her belly again. The faint hint she'd caught yesterday was missing today. Either Nobby had moved further upstream or his scent had been masked by a shift in nature.

They made their way slowly down the slope, following the path run in by the brumbies. A couple of hours later, Meg caught a glimpse of the Chandler River between the trees. And then she caught sight of the brumbies. Slowing to a stop, she held up a finger to her lips, telling Jack to be quiet, then pointed at a clearing below.

The herd moved slowly toward the river, graceful in their wild, dappled beauty, raw vitality surrounding them. Beside her, Jack pulled out his phone and snapped a few shots. Sensing their presence, the herd picked up pace until they galloped away, hooves flying, manes and tails flaring.

"Wow," Jack breathed.

"Beautiful, aren't they?" Awe had stolen her breath too. "If they're still at the river when we get there, the drone would give you amazing footage while we stay a safe distance from them."

His wide grin pressed dimples into his cheeks. "I'll have to shake Nobby's hand for this opportunity, when we find him. That was amazing. I've never been that close to a brumby."

His excitement was tangible, contagious. She wanted to see more of this Jack with his eyes shining and a smile lighting up his face. Although she liked the intense, sexy side of him too. A little too much.

Jack followed Meg through the clearing the brumbies had just vacated, his heart still pounding against his ribs. The brumbies had been beautiful, yes, but the look of enchantment on Meg's face as she'd watched them gallop away had turned him inside out. If love had been a word that existed in his vocabulary, then he'd admit to falling in love with Meg in that moment.

The city, his job, his life on the road — all of it was a distant memory out here in the mountains with Meg. That was another thing that had never happened to him. Never had he been so distracted by anyone that it had made him forget all about his job.

They negotiated rocky outcrops and fallen trees until the forest cleared to give way to the Chandler River. The width of the dried riverbed paid tribute to how high the water might be when in full flow, but for now it was little more than a meandering creek with sunshine sparkling off the water.

"Looks like a great place to launch the drone." Excitement trickled through him. Jack couldn't wait to see the footage the drone would take of a stretch of land he hadn't even known existed. A world he'd never thought he'd be fascinated by.

"It should have a clear flight if we follow the river. With the water level so low and a good portion of the riverbed dry and wide, there's no chance of it getting tangled up anywhere." Meg unhooked a peaked cap from her belt, put it on and pulled her white blonde ponytail through the gap at the back. "We'll take a rest here. Set up the drone. Have something to eat and drink before we follow the river."

"Sounds good."

In a way, she reminded him of a brumby mare. Strong, elegant, wild, beautiful. Admiration flared alongside attraction. Meg had negotiated rocks and rough terrain with the ease and speed of the wild horses that had gone before them. She'd lugged a heavy backpack like it weighed nothing, and surely her shoulders must be aching as much as his were.

Jack slipped his pack off his back and placed it on the ground at his feet. Loosening the straps, he unpacked and set up the drone. When he was done, Meg handed him a sandwich and a canteen of water. They ate and drank, taking in the beauty of the gorge as they sat on a flat boulder.

"That looks like an expensive piece of equipment." Meg nodded toward the drone.

"Top level. It has a range of seven kilometres, so we should get a good stretch of footage on what's ahead."

She slid down off the flat rock and walked to the water's edge. Turning her attention upstream, she closed her eyes and lifted her face to the breeze.

Jack watched, fascinated, as Meg stood in almost a trance-like state for a while. He slipped his phone from his pocket to snap a photo of her, looking for all the world like some vulnerable outback fairy belonging to the waterfall gorge.

That unfamiliar feeling stirred in his chest again. The one that warned him he was getting too close and falling under her spell. He looked down at the picture he'd snapped, banking down the urge to close the distance between them and kiss her until his head spun and her worries about Nobby and Mary, and everything else, melted away.

With a sigh, Jack put his phone away and picked up the remote for the drone instead. He tested it a few times, making it hover and land, flew it a few feet away then back again.

Meg turned away from the water and walked back toward him, an urgency to her step. "Can we send the drone upriver now?"

"Sure." Jack studied the concern on her face for a few seconds. "Everything okay?"

"Yeah ... just ..." Meg twisted the edge of her button-up shirt in her fingers. "It's hard to explain."

"Try me." Whatever was on her mind, it had her tied in knots.

"I've got this gut feeling of urgency. A strong one."

Gut feelings were something Jack was far too familiar with. And even more familiar with how accurate they could be. "Do you think Nobby might be hurt or in danger?" He didn't want to consider the third option. Meg might be tough and resilient, but another death so close to Mary's, on top of everything else she had to deal with, might break her.

"I don't know." She wrapped her arms tightly against her stomach. "I only know we need to hurry."

He reached out and patted her arm. "Then let's line this thing up. We can scan the footage from the control panel as she flies. Does four-kilometre intervals between flights sound fair?"

Meg nodded. "That sounds perfect."

Jack stood beside her as he sent off the drone so that she could see the controller's display screen. The scent of soap on her skin tickled his senses and having her so close heated his blood.

Heads almost touching, they watched the drone

track the river, and looked for signs of life on either side. Nothing except the brumbies crossing the river to the opposite bank with legs, manes and tails flying.

Ten minutes later, he brought the drone back and they gathered their things. Keeping pace with Meg, Jack carried the drone. He wanted to have it ready to take off as soon as they reached the spot where he'd turned it around.

Meg cupped her hands and shouted, "Nobby," her voiced echoing around the gorge. The desperation in her call ate at his gut.

Reaching the turnaround point, Jack set the drone on its way again. Beside him, Meg shifted restlessly from foot to foot as she watched the control screen.

Her breath caught. "There! It's an orange tent."

Jack barely had time to zoom in on the tent before Meg took off at a run. Cursing under his breath and returning the drone, he scrambled everything together to follow her.

Her call for Nobby echoed back at him until he caught up with her metres from where they'd seen the tent. She sprinted between rocks to a flat circle of grass where the tent stood ominously quiet. Her backpack hit the ground with a thump.

"Nobby?" Meg approached the tent cautiously, her steps slow and measured.

A weak moan came from inside the tent. Jack placed the drone on a rock and shrugged off his backpack as she opened the tent zip. The stench of urine and shit leaked out. Jack covered his nose and mouth.

Meg covered hers too. "I'm coming in, Nobby."

She inched into the space barely big enough for two. Jack rolled up the tent flap and secured it, waiting at the entrance.

"What took you so long, girl?" The words were weaker than the old man's groan, barely a whisper inside the tent. A hacking, mucus-filled cough followed them.

Meg knelt beside the sleeping bag and placed her free hand to the man's flushed forehead. "Jesus, Nobby, you're burning up. Jack, there's a first aid kit in my pack. Bring me two paracetamol and some water."

Nobby reached up from the sleeping bag, shivering and shaking. "Don't ... drink ... river water. Infected." His hand was bloody and full of cuts against the sleeve of Meg's shirt.

Meg paled. "Melioidosis?"

"Could be. Dead animals."

Jack's blood ran cold. If they'd run out of the water they'd brought with them, they would have filled up from the river too.

"It's okay, Nobby. We brought fresh water," Meg reassured him. "Jack, there are some latex gloves in the left side pocket of my backpack. Put on a pair and bring me a pair too. And face masks from the first aid kit."

Quickly, Jack retrieved the items and handed them

to Meg. He put on a face mask and then slipped one over her head and secured it over her mouth and nose. She dragged on her gloves and broke the tablets into quarters to make them easier for Nobby to swallow. Jack helped her hold up the old man's head. They had to wait for a break between coughing fits to administer the full dose. Nobby slumped back onto the ground, grey and weak.

"Nobby, how did you get the cuts on your hands?"

"Fell. By the river."

Tears slipped down her cheeks. "Any abdominal pain? Joint pain? Muscle tenderness?"

"Yes." The word fell from Nobby's lips as he drifted into unconsciousness.

"Stay with me, Nobby. Don't you dare leave me!" The panic in Meg's voice ripped a hole in Jack's chest. He already had the satellite phone out when she said, "Call triple zero, Jack. Tell them we have a possible case of pulmonary Melioidosis infection. We've got to get him out of here fast. If he goes deeper into septic shock, we won't be able to save him."

CHAPTER ELEVEN

*M*eg wiped the sweat from Nobby's face with an anti-bacterial towelette from the first aid kit. Guilt gnawed at her stomach. If only she'd come sooner, he wouldn't be in this state. With no way to clean him up, he'd lose his dignity too.

"The SES are on their way from Armidale. They're going to airlift him out. It will be the quickest way. I've given them the coordinates from the drone's memory, so they should find us easily enough." Jack appeared at the entrance to the tent. "What can I do to help?"

"We need to get him out of this sleeping bag and try to cool him down." She reached for a clean-looking towel Nobby had folded in the corner of the tent. "Put this on the grass outside. We'll have to drag him out onto it. I'm sorry, Jack, this won't be pleasant."

His hand touched her shoulder, warm and

comforting, before reaching for the towel. "He'll be okay. We'll do everything we can until the SES arrive."

Meg unzipped the sleeping bag, holding her breath as the stench escaped. Her heart ached for Nobby. He'd hate this so much. "If we can take off his clothes and leave them in the sleeping bag in the tent, everything can be disposed of without spreading too many germs around. I'll need you to lift him."

Jack knelt down and lifted Nobby's shoulders, helping Meg to ease his shirt off. She pushed it to the side of the sleeping bag before removing the rest of Nobby's clothes. She reached for a clean pair of underwear. It was the best she could do to help him retain some dignity.

Jack eased him out of the tent onto the towel, limp and drifting in and out of consciousness. Meg retrieved more towelettes from her backpack and cleaned him up as best she could. The moist cloths would at least help cool his feverish skin in the absence of water. She dressed him in the clean underwear while Jack dribbled water from the canteen into his mouth during his bouts of consciousness.

In silence, they tended to Nobby, Meg lost track of time as the sun crept toward the west.

"We'll need to let the ranger know about the contamination." Meg sat back in a crouch to change her gloves, sadness mixing with exhaustion and worry.

"Already done. He's on his way too. With a clean-up crew. Everything in Nobby's tent will be incinerated."

Nobby reached for Meg, his hand shaky. "Mary's ring."

His words were so faint, she struggled to hear them. "Where is it?"

"Pillow."

"The sleeping bag pillow." Jack stood and reached into the tent, retrieving the ring from under the pillow. He pressed it into Nobby's palm and curled his fingers around it. "Here you go."

Meg fell in love with Jack a little more. "Thank you."

His bone-melting smile brought light to the grim situation. He brushed away a tear on her cheek with this thumb, then held her close. "You're welcome."

She absorbed his warmth and comfort until the distant whir of a chopper grew louder. Relief flooded Meg. "They're coming."

Nobby opened his eyes. He reached for Jack's hand, pressed the ring into it. "Keep it ... safe ... for Meg."

Panic gripped Meg's throat as Nobby's eyes drifted closed again, his chest barely lifting with every rattled breath. "We're going to get you out of here. You will be okay." He had to be.

A small team of SES members, led by the ranger, burst into the clearing. A blur of activity ensued until the chopper hovered above, a paramedic descending with the stretcher.

Numb, curled into the comfort of Jack's side, with the weight of his arm around her, Meg watched them secure Nobby and lift him away. As the chopper disappeared toward Armidale, the ranger approached them.

"We'll finish cleaning up here. You'll want to get to the hospital."

"Thank you." The long hike back out the gorge stretched ahead when all she'd wanted to do was get in that helicopter with Nobby. If he didn't make it ...

Jack gave her a quick hug before releasing her. "I'll pack up the drone and get our things together."

Life turned to slow motion, an endless blur of trees, rocks and slopes. Jack's firm hand on her arm, guiding her over the same outcrops she'd sprinted over earlier. A flicker of relief touched her belly when the service road eventually came into view just as the sky took on the hues of sunset.

He eased her backpack off her shoulders, lifted her into his arms and placed her on the seat of the Pajero. "Put your seatbelt on."

She obeyed, that same sense of urgency she'd felt entering the gorge chasing away the numbness. "Hurry, Jack," she urged as he slipped into the driver's seat after stowing their gear in the back.

They made it to the hospital in record time, but the emergency department staff sent them to the waiting room where they sat until the world beyond the windows went dark and the streetlights came on.

She called Aunty Phyl on her mobile, listened to the cheers of the crowd in the Riverside Pub and fielded the questions about Nobby's condition with a promise to keep everyone updated.

Jack held her hand tight, brought her coffee, watched her pace, offered his shoulder for her to rest on when her eyes grew too heavy to keep open.

"Miss Moonie?"

Meg's eyes snapped open. Her face was buried in Jack's neck, her butt firmly settled in his lap, and his arms were locked securely around her. Placing a hand on his chest, she pushed herself up to look at the emergency room doctor.

"Yes?" Her heart pounded against her rib cage, what-ifs cluttering her mind.

"You can see Mr Wilkie for a few minutes. He's not out of danger yet, but we've administered a strong antibiotic that should do the trick. With plenty of rest and fluids, his chances are looking pretty good."

Meg eased out of Jack's arms to stand. She longed for a shower, so the sluice of hot water could wash away the grime and aches of the day. "That's good news."

"Come along, I'll take you both in." The doctor led the way to Nobby's room.

He'd never been a big man, but lying against the stark white hospital sheets Nobby looked incredibly small and weak. The cracks that had slowly been forming in Meg's strength crumbled at the sight of a man usually so full of life reduced to a sickly mess of oxygen masks, beeping monitors and intravenous drips.

Right there was the reason she could never leave Bindarra Creek, not even for a little while. She loved her people too much. Yet slowly, one by one, age and illness were stealing them from her. All the more reason why she had to bring new life to the town.

Meg crossed the floor to the bed and took Nobby's hand in hers. His fingers were cold and his skin so much cooler than it had been down in the gorge. "How long will he be in hospital?"

The doctor flicked through Nobby's chart from the basket at the head of the bed, ticked a few boxes and checked the IV lines. "As soon as he's rehydrated and we're sure the antibiotics are effective, we'll release him. About a week, I'd say."

Nobby would hate that. "Can we have him transferred to the Bindarra Creek Hospital? I'm sure he'd like to be closer to home."

"I'd say that's a strong possibility. I'll check if they have the facilities available for his treatment." The doctor smiled. "As long as there is someone to keep an eye on him when he's released. It will take a while for him to get his strength back."

Meg smiled. Between Aunty Phyllis and the ladies of the CWA, they'd bully and nurture him back to health, in that order. "I think we're pretty safe there."

"Good. I'll leave you with him for a few minutes then." He eyed both Jack and Meg. "And then I'd suggest you both find something to eat and a nice comfortable place to sleep for the night. You've had a big day. I can recommend Amity House, a bed and breakfast on Faulkner Street. They'll take you in."

"Thank you." Meg wasn't sure she could eat or sleep.

"He was lucky the two of you found him when you did. In another day or so, he might not have been so lucky. The infection spread quickly." The doctor looked at Jack. "A far cry from the usual situations you find yourself in, Mr Hughes."

Beside Meg, Jack stiffened. "A little."

"It's a good thing rumours and viral videos quickly lose footing in this modern world. Always something new and more exciting to gossip over." He nodded and smiled as he made his way out the door. "The SES will have footage of the rescue. Might be a little positive exposure for you. The media is bound to get hold of the news of the Melioidosis scare, so no doubt it will be aired on the late news tonight." The ward door closed behind him.

Jack cringed. He hadn't given thought to the fact that the media might pick up on the infection scare and that he'd been right bang in the middle of it. He'd been too wrapped up in the rescue and Meg to think about it. With a little luck, the doctor had been wrong and it hadn't been newsworthy enough. Beside him, Meg swayed on her feet.

"Why don't we let Nobby sleep, and come back to see him tomorrow?" He steadied her with a hand on her back.

"Yes, a good night's sleep will do him good."

And because she seemed reluctant to leave, Jack gave her hand a little tug. "Let's go find this Amity House. We'll book a room and find something to eat."

"Okay." She pressed a kiss to Nobby's forehead and gave his hand a little squeeze. "We'll be back in the morning, Nobby."

Nobby's eyes fluttered open. He lifted his oxygen mask away from his face a little. "Forever."

"Forever?" Meg leaned down to hear him.

"She ... promised me ... forever. Mary." A tear leaked down his cheek.

Meg curled her fingers around his hand. "It's okay. Don't upset yourself. We can talk about this when you're better."

"No." He hacked out a cough that shook his frame. "Didn't murder Mary."

"I know that."

"Mistake."

"What was a mistake?" Intrigued, Jack shifted closer, his gut instincts scrambling as he recognised a story.

"Oleander. Medicine. To help her skin."

Jack looked at Meg, eyebrow raised. She shook her head. "Mary had eczema. Nobby often used to make up herbal pastes and swabs to stop the itching."

"Made a pot. Oleander tea. Meant for paste mix." He dropped the oxygen mask back into place for a few breaths. "Drank the wrong tea."

Meg sagged against Jack. "Oh, Nobby."

Exhausted by his confession, Nobby slipped back into sleep. For a moment, they stood and watched his chest rise and fall, the beep of the heart monitor staying steady in the room.

Shock made Meg's skin almost translucent under the harsh fluorescent lights. She trembled against him and he steadied her with his hands.

"Meg, he's delirious with fever. He could be mistaken." Jack tried to reassure her, but the wheels turned inside his mind, churning out all the questions he'd like to ask.

Meg shook her head. "It makes sense. There were two pots of herbal tea on the cooktop that day. I'll have to tell Riley."

"Let's find out the facts first. Nobby is in no state for a confession. He's heavily medicated and has suffered a trauma. Wait until he's a little stronger and thinking more clearly."

In the past, he would have jumped on that confession and turned it into a story, with no hesitation. But with Nobby lying breaths away from death, and the stricken look on Meg's face, he called for his instincts to settle. She mattered too much for him to allow his reporter's instinct to take over.

"It's late, Meg. We're tired and worn out. Nobby isn't going anywhere tonight, or tomorrow. As soon as he's stronger, we can get the full story out of him."

Jack led her to the door, down the corridor and out to the car park. He helped her into the car then climbed in himself. A sharp jab dug into his thigh and he remembered the ring Nobby had given him. Mary's ring. He'd been insistent that Jack take care of it. *Keep it safe. For Meg.*

She was silent all the way to Amity House. Said nothing as he booked rooms with the friendly owner and didn't even twitch when the woman said they only had one room left, although it had twin beds.

When he'd asked where they could get some food, the woman had looked at their crumpled clothing and tired faces with a soft smile and said, "Perhaps you should eat in your room. I have leftover casserole from dinner. Why don't I warm it up and bring it to you?"

"Thank you. That's very kind of you."

Relief shifted through him. He took the key for the room and led Meg up the stairs. Under different circumstances, he would have taken the time to admire the expertise in the woodwork or the period features that lent character to the old house. But tonight, all he wanted was to lie down, hold Meg in his arms and help her forget the horrors she'd seen and heard today.

Reaching the room, he steered her inside, sat her on the bed and loosened her boots. "Why don't you find a clean set of clothes and take the first shower? You're dead on your feet."

She nodded, moving with robotic movements as she found clothes. The bathroom door closed behind her. He could hear her crying, his own heart breaking. It took all the willpower he had not to walk into the bathroom to comfort her. He was in too deep already.

Their hostess delivered the piping hot casserole in a dish, with two plates and cutlery on a tray as Meg came out the shower. It would stay hot until he'd scrubbed himself clean.

He showered, they ate, everything around them surreal in a haze of exhaustion. Jack placed the tray outside the room door for collection as instructed. When he came back inside, Meg had turned down the covers and curled up in a ball on the bed with her back to him.

"Meg?" His heart ached for her. So many shocks in such a short time. His outback fairy was broken, the magical smile gone from her lips.

Her shoulders shook. "Mary didn't have to die. It was all a stupid mistake."

Jack lay down on the bed and gathered her close until he spooned around her. He had no words to answer the truth, so held her tight against him until her tears were spent and she slipped into sleep.

With a sigh, he pulled the covers up over them and

waited for sleep to come to him. It didn't. Somewhere around midnight, her whisper reached him.

"Jack?"

"Meg."

She turned over until she faced him, her head pillowed on his arm. He could barely make out her features in the darkened room, but he knew that even ravaged by tears, she'd be beautiful.

"Thank you."

"For what?"

"For staying with me, for helping me with Nobby." She reached out to run her palm over his face. "I like you, Jack. You're a good man. In here." Her hand covered his heart, cool against the warmth of his skin. "I'm sorry for the waterworks. I'm not usually a crier."

Her touch made his heart do crazy leaps. He wanted to hold her tight, love her hard, ease her pain. "It's been a rough day. Things haven't been easy for you."

Jack gathered her closer against him. What Meg had to deal with made his own troubles pale. The hype over the viral video would die down eventually. He could recover his reputation when the truth came out. But Meg could never get back what she'd lost. He'd never loved anyone the way Meg loved her people. But then, he'd also never felt for anyone the way he felt about her.

Her fingers trailed down his chest and traced a path to his hip. He sucked in a breath as they skimmed the waistband of his boxer shorts, coming to rest on his thigh.

Her lips skimmed his jaw and he lost the willpower to evade them, so when her mouth searched for his, he kissed her. A slow exploration, losing himself in her taste and the magic of her mouth. He'd never fallen in love with a flavour before.

The thought slipped into subconsciousness as need overrode it with the play of her hands on his back. She breathed his name into his neck as she burrowed into him. Tenderness flooded him, another rare emotion for Jack. Meg was dynamite and he wanted to be the only man who held the trigger.

He rolled onto his back, bringing her with him until her body aligned with his, and every inch of her touched him. He wanted the barrier of clothing gone from between them. Every part of him ached for the touch and taste of her skin.

She lifted her face to look at him, moved against him in a slow dance of invitation Jack was powerless to resist. Her fairy green gaze held his captive and he lost himself in the depths of it. And when she eased herself up, straddled him and removed her T-shirt, Jack reached for his wallet and the protection inside, knowing there'd be no regrets tonight.

CHAPTER TWELVE

*E*very inch of her skin burned with a fever only Jack could remedy. His hands, his mouth, his body — all of them belonged to her tonight, whatever dawn chose to bring.

They moved in perfect unison, a slow match to the flame, until the fire grew out of control, gathered speed, and consumed them. In its wake, they lay spent, Jack's arms anchored around her, his chest rising and falling under her.

Meg rested her cheek against him and listened to the unsteady pounding of his heart. When Jack walked away, she wouldn't be left unscathed. He'd take a large chunk of her heart with him. She could dream that he'd stay, but the reality was that Jack was a man of a world much bigger than hers.

Could she be a part of that world? When Aunty Phyl and Nobby, and all the people she cared about, were gone and she was alone in Bindarra Creek with the museum, would she regret letting Jack leave town?

With a sigh, Meg closed her eyes. Counting her chickens before they got an invitation into the coop would get her nowhere. Jack didn't seem like the kind of man who promise forever. He had dragons to slay and worlds to conquer, stories to uncover and tell. She had Granny Mary's museum and a dream to keep alive.

Jack's fingers tangled in her hair, massaged her scalp while his other hand drew circles at the base of her spine. The shift of his body said they weren't done yet, only resting.

She could dream of that promise of forever, or she could live for the moment and enjoy Jack while she had him. Life was too short for wishes of what might be or what could have been. As his hands made magic on her skin again and his body came alive under her touch, she knew she had now, and it had to be enough.

Dawn broke behind the thin curtains on the window as Jack slept beside her. She never wanted to leave his side, but reality beckoned only a few kilometres down the road where Nobby lay ill in a hospital bed.

Slipping out from under Jack's arm, she tiptoed into the bathroom to shower and brush her teeth. Wrapped in a towel, she sat on the edge of the bath to call the hospital and check on Nobby. Surely if there'd been a problem, they would have called her? No calls or messages meant that hopefully Nobby had had a good night.

She got through to find that he'd been moved out of ICU into a private ward.

"He's a tough one," the nurse told her. "The antibiotics are working well, but the doctor is still a bit concerned about the fluid on his lungs. He'll talk to you about that when you get here later this morning." And that's all she'd say because hospitals had protocols.

Meg sighed as she stood up and opened the bathroom door. Jack sat on the edge of the mattress, running a hand through his bed hair.

"Hey." A cheeky grin spread his lips as he took in the towel tucked in securely above her breasts.

"Morning." Shyness crept in as she remembered how she'd let go of all inhibition in Jack's arms last night.

He patted the mattress beside him. "Did I hear you calling the hospital? How's Nobby?"

She sat, the dip of the mattress tipping them closer together. "Much better this morning."

"That's great news." He pressed a kiss to her shoulder, before turning her face to his. "Mmm, you smell so good. Good morning." His lips touched hers, the movement fleeting. "I think I'm in a spot of trouble here, Meg."

A flush rose on her skin. "What kind of trouble, Jack?"

"I think I'm falling in love with a spirit of the

outback." His mouth teased the spot where her pulse ticked in her neck. He gave it a little nip. "I can't get enough of you. I'm bewitched."

Meg arched her neck, allowing his mouth access to wherever it wanted to go. Her heart pounded, leaving her speechless. She didn't want empty declarations of love, but from Jack's lips it sounded genuine and heartfelt. How long would bewitchment last? Would it last long enough to break her heart when duty called him away again?

The towel gave way to his hands. Meg gave way to the magic of his touch. Together, they rode wave after wave of sensation until the flame flared and then settled to a glow again.

Spent, she lay in his arms, reluctant to leave as she cuddled into his side. A warm, safe place to be. A low hum filtered into the room as the air conditioning kicked in, signalling the start to the day at Amity House.

"Have you ever thought beyond the job, Jack? To what you'd do if you didn't get it back?"

He hooked one arm up behind his head, held her a little tighter with the other. "If you'd asked me that question a few days ago, I would have said I'd do anything to get my job back. I didn't do what that girl is accusing me of. It wasn't me in that video. I'm not a player, Meg."

"I believe you." The conviction in his words was enough.

With a sigh, he eased away from her and sat on the edge of the bed again. "I will fight until I'm cleared of those accusations and the truth comes out. There was never any doubt in my mind that I would get my job back. The question in my mind now is if I want it back."

Meg's heart skipped a beat as she pushed up to sit against the headboard, her legs stretched out in front of her. "What would you do if you didn't go back?"

He looked back at her and grinned. "Maybe the *Bindarra Bugle* needs a roving reporter."

Hope flared and died again. "I'm not sure reports of infected water, flood, drought and dying country towns will be enough for you. You're a good, well-known, international correspondent. You didn't even want this assignment."

"That was before I met you." The grin slipped, turning his expression serious. "I mean that, Meg. Talking to the people in Bindarra Creek, rescuing Nobby down in that gorge, seeing everything the community does to help keep the town alive ... it's an eye-opener for city people like me. Sometimes we can't see the struggle on our own doorstep. I'd like to be a part of that."

Doubt weighed like a stone in her gut. "Would it be enough for you?"

"I don't know." He lay back until his head was in her lap. "How do we ever know if we're making the right choices?"

"We don't. But sometimes we have to go with our gut." Meg smoothed out the untidy spikes her fingers had made in his hair.

Jack eased himself up on his elbow, tugged her toward him and kissed her hard. "My gut says a shower is in order. Together. To save water, of course." His trademark cheeky grin returned. "Then we'll have breakfast and go see Nobby."

"Whatever happens, Jack, I know you'll make the right decision." Meg smiled, her heart full of love. She hoped Aunty Phyl had a stash of cigars and champagne to share with her when he broke it.

Jack drove the short distance to the Armidale Public Hospital with too much on his mind. Whatever magic Meg possessed, she'd scrambled his brain cells. He'd actually given thought to quitting his job while he'd listened to Meg's muted voice talking to the hospital from the bathroom. Could he survive in a small town like Bindarra Creek?

He cast a glance at Meg. He'd never had sex that blew his mind and made him think that maybe this girl could be the one. Until last night. And this morning. Twice. Each time rocking his world harder than before.

He'd fallen hard and fast. For her courage and commitment, the way she went all in for those she cared about, her kindness and caring nature. Her beauty, inside and out. Meg Moonie was unlike anyone he'd ever met, and for the first time ever, he'd met someone he wanted to keep in his life forever.

But when that first flush was over, would his feet itch to be on the move the way they had with Kelsey? Could he leave Meg behind in Bindarra Creek when the story bug bit?

She'd asked him if being part of the community would be enough. He tried to envision himself working for the *Bindarra Bugle*, covering local stories from behind a desk instead of covering international stories from in front of a camera. Any thought of staying in one place for any length of time usually gave him chills. There was no sign of those chills, and that scared the crap out of him.

Jack found a parking spot and eased the Pajero into it. He opened Meg's door and helped her down, her hand slipping into his as he locked the car and they walked toward the hospital entrance. He could get used to that. Her hand in his.

Reaching Nobby's room, they found him sleeping, his breathing more even, less rattly, and a little colour back in his face. The oxygen mask had been replaced with a tube to his nose.

Meg leaned over to press a kiss to the old man's forehead. "Hey, sleepyhead."

Nobby's eyes drifted open, a weak smile appearing. "Meg." His voice came through as dry and cracked as his lips.

"You're looking a lot better this morning."

"Feeling better." His gaze wandered to Jack. "Who's this?"

"Jack Hughes. He's the one doing the story on the museum. Do you remember what happened yesterday?"

"Yes. The water. Made me sick."

"Jack helped me find you. We used a drone." Meg smiled up at Jack, making his heart jump. "Nobby loves gadgets. Do you want to tell him about the drone while I go and find the doctor in charge?"

"I can do that." He also had to give the man Mary's ring back.

"Good. I'll be back in a tick." Her hand slipped from his, leaving his fingers still tingling from her touch.

Jack watched her walk out the door until a dry chuckle, followed by a raspy cough brought his attention back to Nobby.

"Sweet girl."

Jack agreed. "Nobby, yesterday you gave me a ring. Mary's ring."

"Keep it safe. For Meg. Mary wanted it."

"Wanted her to have the ring?"

"Yes. Commitment ring." The old man's eyes fluttered closed for a second. "I trust you. Mary said ... you'd be a good man. The man. For Meg."

Okay, that made his gut twist into a knot of what-the-fuck. He touched a hand to the station ID around his neck where the ring sat securely attached to the lanyard. "You don't even know me. How do you know you can trust me?"

"Mary knew you. She'd seen you before."

Jack rocked back on his heels. The man had to be running a fever because he sure as hell made no sense. Yet Meg had said something similar down in Mary's cellar that day.

"Don't give it to her yet. You'll know. When the time is right." A sigh rattled from Nobby's chest and he seemed to drift off into sleep again.

Questions churned through Jack's mind. He'd been set up once before. What were the chances that this might be another scam? He had a ring in his possession that belonged to a dead woman, given to him by a man under suspicion of her murder, who'd barely survived a trip to Hell contracting an infection from drinking poisoned water. Summing it up made his head throb. Jack pulled a chair closer to the bed.

The scrape of the chair legs against the floor had Nobby's eyes fluttering open again. "Tell me ... about the drone."

Jack talked about the footage they'd recorded, how they'd found Nobby and the rescue that had followed. Talked until Meg came back into the room and Nobby's snore matched the rasp of his breathing. Talked so he wouldn't think too much and freak himself out over what Nobby had said about Mary.

He stood so Meg could sit, then perched on the armrest beside her. "What did the doctor say?"

"Nobby should be strong enough to be transferred to the hospital in Bindarra Creek tomorrow. He'll feel better closer to home and his friends."

"That's great." He twisted a length of her hair around his finger then let it slide away.

"How's he been?" She leaned into him as he stretched his arm along the back of the chair, angling his body closer.

He liked being close to her with her perfume chasing the scary questions from his head and replacing them with pleasant ones instead. "Talkative."

Meg smiled. "That's Nobby for you." She placed a hand on his thigh. "Riley Morgan is on his way in. He rang to say he'd be here in about half an hour."

"Couldn't the investigation wait until Nobby is transferred?" Surely they could give the poor old guy one more day to gain his strength.

"Riley's keen to get things cleared up. I still can't believe it was a simple mistake. Poor Nobby."

She'd cried her tears in Jack's arms last night. All that was left now was sadness and regret. "It will take time, Meg, but everything will be okay."

"I know. But Nobby has a way to go yet to be cleared of any charges. Riley's confident the coroner will rule it out as accidental, but he still has to close the case."

CHAPTER THIRTEEN

*A*week had never felt so long, despite busy planning during the daylight hours and languorous nights spent in Jack's arms.

Meg sorted through the old war letters donated by Rob and Lyn Stone at the post office across the road. How easily important information got lost. If Rob hadn't removed the old wooden pigeonholes to install a new sorting system, they'd never have found years of missing history in the letters from World War II, written by a handful of soldiers who sadly hadn't returned to the fold.

Nobby was finally due to arrive at the Bindarra Creek Hospital today, after being kept in Armidale for longer than expected. He'd needed stronger antibiotics to curb the infection and a little longer for observation.

Jack and Bennie had been out on the town

conducting interviews and filming segments for the program.

A smile teased Meg's lips. The town's upcoming five minutes of fame had everyone excited and energised. The streets of Bindarra Creek hadn't looked so cheerful since Christmas and New Year's Eve. With Valentine's Day only days away, the florist had a colourful array of flowers out on display on the pavement, kept fresh with a fine spray mist Jon Johnson had rigged up outside.

Over at the Cyprus Café, the CWA committee sipped coffee and tea as they finalised the plans for Saturday's Valentine's Day Ball, all dressed up for Bennie's camera.

At the front counter in the museum shop, Aunty Phyl rocked a 1960s dress she'd found relatively unscathed in the storeroom, and she'd styled her hair into a beehive. She'd dusted and polished everything in the old show cabinets until they gleamed in the sunlight from the newly washed windows.

Jack had fixed the hinges on the museum door and repaired the leaning verandah post but painting the old shop would have to wait. Chelsea Morgan — soon to be Sullivan — had donated some leftover cans of soft olive green paint that would look great on the door, window frames and fascia boards. With luck there'd be enough for the newly repaired verandah posts.

Bennie had helped her clean and set up the old kitchen out the back of the shop with displays so Jack could interview her and Aunty Phyl in it. Not the ideal room of choice, but the only one that hadn't sustained a lot of water damage on the ceiling and walls from the burst pipe.

A mannequin stood over a pot on the old Aga stove, wooden spoon in hand, her 1800s dress covered with an apron to hide the rusty watermarks. Her wig, donated by Edwina, had been neatly tied in a bun and topped with a mob cap.

Another mannequin had been dressed in a suit and sat on a worn tapestry chair by the gleaming fireplace, reading a book with his glasses perched on his nose. He wore a cap on his head to cover the fact that 'he' was actually 'she' because the male mannequin had been beyond repair.

Aunty Phyl had polished up an old walnut bookcase with bevelled, leadlight glass doors and filled it with a collection of fragile leather-bound books, adding to the cosy ambience of the scene.

Meg tied the war letters back up in string and set them on the oak roll-top writing desk next to the fountain pen and inkpot before running her hands over the smooth wood. Jack's arms came around her from behind and his lips nuzzled her neck.

"You smell like beeswax and dust."

She closed her eyes and leaned back against him, her hands anchoring his arms in place. God, she loved Jack. Every inch, every muscle, everything Jack. "Hey, you." She tilted her head to meet the magic of his searching mouth and let herself fall into his kiss.

Coming up for air, he said, "The ambulance has arrived at the hospital. Nobby's home."

The churn in her belly settled. "Is Riley there?" The sergeant hadn't been able to interview Nobby in Armidale after all. He'd been too sick to speak, his lungs unable to sustain his breath for long enough.

"Yeah. That's why I came to tell you. You should be there with him." He slipped his arms from around her. "Bennie and I are going to take a break from filming if you'd like me to come with you."

"Thanks."

Relief flooded her. It was nice to have someone to lean on, and every minute left with Jack counted. Neither of them had raised the subject of what-ifs in the lead up to the end of his stay in Bindarra Creek. Not yet. The flicker of hope in her heart wanted him to have found what he was looking for in their town.

"Bennie's waiting for us at the hospital. Nobby got a hero's welcome home with everyone out on the streets for filming."

"He'd be very embarrassed." Meg turned to face Jack, slipping her hand into his. "Does Aunty Phyl know?"

"Yeah, gave her the news on the way in. She'll lock up the shop and come down with us."

On cue, Aunty Phyl called, "Let's go, lovebirds."

Meg and Jack walked into the shop to find Aunty

Phyl cutting open a box of six champagne bottles.

"Champagne? Are we celebrating Nobby's return, Aunty Phyl?"

She cast a wary glance at Jack. "We're either celebrating a coming home or commiserating a leaving town or maybe both. Depends on what happens next. Either way, I want to be prepared."

Meg held back a sigh. It was probably selfish of her not to want to think past one day at a time. "Come on, let's go see Nobby. I'll help you stock the fridge when we get back from the hospital." She held out her free hand to help her aunt up from her kneeling position.

They left the museum, pausing to lock the door. The recent spate of crime had everyone a little nervous still. Aunty Phyl led the way as they crossed Main Street at the cenotaph, passed Lette Park, waved to a group of veterans heading into the RSL for lunch, and walked on to the hospital.

Bennie sat waiting on the low wall outside, camera at his feet. He gave Aunty Phyl a wave as she strolled past him into the cool interior of the hospital to find out where they'd taken Nobby.

"Senior Sergeant Morgan arrived behind the ambulance. He's inside." Bennie nodded his head in the direction Aunty Phyl had taken.

Meg quelled the stab of irritation, reminding herself that Riley was only doing his job. "He'll want to wrap this case up quickly and stamp out any unnecessary gossip and concerns."

Jack's fingers tightened around hers as he tugged her toward the doors. "Let's see what's going on. Nobby needs his family."

The receptionist at the desk directed them to Nobby's ward, but they had no trouble locating it as Aunty Phyl's raised voice reached their ears. "Riley Morgan, I paddled your backside with your mother's permission for throwing stones when you were a kid and I'll paddle it again now if you're suggesting what I think you're suggesting."

As they stopped in the doorway, Meg noticed Riley put a soothing hand on her aunt's arm. The rumble of his voice was low. "Give me a chance to do my job, Ms Moonie."

"Settle down, Phyl. Or I'll call the nurse to throw you out. The boy's got to ask questions." A cough rattled Nobby's chest. "I've got nothing to hide. They can put me on a lie detector if they need to."

"That won't be necessary, Nobby. Just tell me what happened as you remember it." Riley turned to face Meg as they entered the room. "Hi, Meg. Hughes." He shook his head at Bennie. "Bergman, you'd better not be rolling that camera."

Bennie lifted it from his shoulder. "No, sir. It's off. See?"

Riley looked and nodded, satisfied the camera was turned off. He faced Nobby again. "Are you okay with everyone being in the room?"

"I've got nothing to hide, son." Nobby repeated

what he'd told Meg and Jack at the hospital in Armidale about the two pots of tea on the cooktop.

Riley checked the notes on his tablet. "That ties up. We took two pots of brew for testing." He asked more questions, giving Nobby plenty of time to answer, then stabbed the point of his pen on the tablet glass. "I'll go back to the station and write up my report for the coroner."

Meg's heart sat at the base of her throat, jamming her airways as she sucked in a breath and counted the squares on the tiled floor to give her a chance to herd her fears. "Will you be laying charges, Riley? Please, be honest with me."

Riley sighed. "Meg, it's up to the coroner on this one, but I'd say there's a good chance he'll rule Mary's death as accidental. Unless …?" His pause had her eyes snapping to his.

"God no, Riley." Her heart sank at the thought. "We won't be laying any charges. Will we, Aunty Phyl?"

Phyl shook her head, her eyes a little teary. "It was all a horrible mistake. Nobby, we're going to have to invest in a labelling machine for your brews."

"Good idea, Phyl." Nobby did nothing to stem the tears that flowed down his cheek and onto the pillow. "Doesn't mend the fact that it was my fault. I as good as killed her. You should lay charges."

Meg released her grip on Jack's hand and went to stand beside the bed. She pulled a tissue from the box and dabbed at his cheeks. "No. It's okay, Nobby. You are family, we'll get through this. Mary would not have wanted you to blame yourself."

Riley cleared his throat. "I'll leave you all alone now." He shook Nobby's hand and turned to leave just as Jack's phone rang.

Jack dragged his phone out of his pocket and checked the number. *Shit.* He cast Meg an apologetic glance before stepping out into the hallway to answer. "Hang on a minute," he said into the phone and made his way out of the hospital to sit on the wall where Bennie had waited earlier. "Kelsey. What's up?" He was almost too afraid to ask as he waited for a barrage of anger to break forth from the phone.

"Jack, I owe you an apology."

"A what?"

"An apology." Her breath shuddered out down the line. "Has Darren called you?"

"No." He hadn't heard a peep out of his producer, but then Channel Eight and its high pressure environment seemed like a different planet right now. "Why?"

"Well, I'm sitting here with a very personal letter on my desk from Tamryn Hollister." Nerves gave way to bemusement in her voice.

Jack didn't stem his groan. What had the little tyke

done now?

"No, this is good, Jack. It's an apology and a sworn statement that absolves you of any blame or involvement in that damn video. I'm sure you'll receive one too. It's probably in your letterbox at the apartment. Would you like me to go and check?"

Jack dragged a hand over his face. "No, it can wait until I get back to town." If she went there now, she'd likely be carried away by the smell of half-empty beer bottles and decomposing garbage, because he'd left town in a hurry. "Kelsey, does this mean ...?" He was too afraid to voice the question lodged in his throat, positive he wouldn't like the answer.

She laughed. He waited for the tingle the sound usually brought to his blood. Nothing. *Nada.*

"No, Jack. This isn't an attempt at reconciliation. I think we're both smart enough to know that it was over between us long before the Hollister girl and her shenanigans. I just wanted to say sorry about the way I reacted. I should have trusted you and I shouldn't have taken my frustration out on Betty's fender. It was just ... the final straw at the time, you know?"

He did know because if he were totally honest with himself, he'd have to admit that he'd been looking for a way out of the dead end relationship with Kelsey. He'd known they were moving in different directions. He'd just not been ready to admit it and neither had she.

"Say something, Jack."

"God, Kelsey. Did we fuck up by leaving it to fester

for so long?"

"No, we were too comfortable, that's all. I think what we had had run its course and it ended in the worst possible way. I'll pay to get Betty's fender fixed."

"You don't have to do that. Look, Kelsey ... I've met someone. And I think ... I think she might be special."

"In *Bindarra Creek*?" The shock in her voice carried clearly down the line.

Jack bristled. "Don't say it like that. They're really nice people out here."

"I'm sure they are, Mr Defensive. What I meant was: she's a country girl, you're a city boy with itchy feet. How would you make it work? Unless she's willing to move to the city? Are you sure this isn't a rebound thing?"

Was it? "I don't know what it is. I've never felt anything like this."

"Oh, Jack ..." He could hear the smile in her voice. "Well, I think you've got a few choices to make."

Choices. Isn't that what Edwina Lette had said? His smile widened. "I guess I have."

"Choose carefully, you don't want to break any more hearts. Are we good, Jack? Friends?"

"Always friends."

"Good. If ever you need a favour, I'm here for you."

"Thanks." He hung up with a promise to keep her updated just as Meg walked out into the sunshine.

"Everything okay?" Concern lit her beautiful eyes.

"Yeah, all good. That was Kelsey, my ex. Tamryn

Hollister has written an apology for that viral video."

Meg sat on the wall beside him. "That's good news, right?"

"Sure is." So why didn't it feel like it? He'd wanted his name cleared so he could get back out in the field, get back to work, but the itch that normally drove his feet into action appeared to be missing.

"Then why so glum?"

Good question. Maybe because with his name cleared, there was no reason to hang around in Bindarra Creek. He should be dancing in the street, when instead the news weighed like concrete on his mind.

"I guess it will take time for the news to sink in." Jack shrugged. "How is Nobby doing?"

"Much better physically. Mentally, not so good. He's taking it really hard. It's not going to be easy or quick to heal knowing Granny's death was his mistake. It seems so unfair. But Nobby is our family too and we'll work through it, one step at a time."

Jack leaned in and nudged her shoulder with his. "If I take away anything from this town, it's that nothing can break the bond this community has. I've never experienced anything like that." He watched Florrie Miller walk toward them with a gift hamper in her hands.

She stopped in front of them. "Meg, Jack. I've got a little something from the CWA for Nobby. Is it okay to go in?"

"Of course, Mrs Miller. Just stop by the nurses' station to check with them first. He's in Ward 2C."

"He's not contagious, is he?"

"Not at all." Meg reached out to pat Florrie's hand. "It'll be fine. Go on. And thank you, he'll appreciate the gift."

"Well, since my husband can't make it, I'll say a little prayer for Nobby too."

"He'd like that, thank you."

Florrie bustled away and disappeared through the glass doors. Jack shook his head. "Growing up in boarding school, I always thought of the students and staff as my family, my community, but no one ever made nice gestures like that. Not even on birthdays."

"You grew up in a different world. Here there is a lifetime of history passed down from generation to generation. Everyone is connected in some way, since the day the town grew and expanded out of a trading post. All over Australia are towns like ours, where family is more than just blood ties. I'm sorry you never experienced that, Jack. It's that relationship that has given this town the strength to survive."

He loved the passion in her eyes, the conviction in her voice. He loved everything about Meg. Jack cupped her face in his hands and pressed a lingering kiss to her lips. When he got the call from Darren, would he be able to walk away and leave her behind? The thought burned like acid in his gut.

CHAPTER FOURTEEN

*I*n the garden at the side of the museum, Meg put a final coat of grapeseed oil onto the wooden hitch of the old seeder donated by the Sullivan family. The rusty iron wheels had cleaned up nicely and she'd repaired the seed box on the rear as best she could. Nobby would be proud of her efforts when he saw them. She hoped that if Granny was watching, she would be too. Confidence flared that with Jack and Bennie's help, the dream grant would be a reality after all.

Jack. Meg's tummy did a little somersault. With the filming and interviews for the program wrapping up, she'd soon have to prepare her heart to say goodbye. When he returned to the city and his busy work life, he'd soon forget about Bindarra Creek, about her. Maybe not immediately, but with time and distance, the chance of them growing apart was high. Especially since they hadn't discussed the future.

A sigh escaped her lips as she lay down the brush, screwed the cap back onto the oil bottle and placed it on the old, round cast iron table. Was this the kind of love that lasted forever? Or was it just a pleasant fling with no regrets at the end of it? The Moonie women appeared to have a lot in common with the Venn women. The men in their life didn't like to hang around. They tended to fall for happy wanderers.

Yet Meg had never loved Logan the way she loved Jack. She'd been hurt by Logan, yes. But the thought of watching Jack walk away and never seeing him again filled her heart with aching emptiness.

Could she leave Bindarra Creek, Aunty Phyl, Nobby and all the people she loved so much, to follow Jack around the world? Travel would be nice, but this town was her life. But there she went counting chickens before the eggs had even been laid. As much as she wanted Jack to stay, she'd never try to tie him down against his will.

Meg pushed through the garden gate, out onto the pavement in front of the museum entrance. She sat on Granny Mary's park bench to take in the activity around her.

Across the road, Jack interviewed Rob and Lyn outside the post office. Her heart fluttered against her rib cage. God, he was so damn gorgeous in his red polo shirt and black jeans. His city-styled hair had grown longer since he'd been in town, lending him a sexy, slightly untamed look.

Aunty Phyl's heels clacked against the concrete as the newly installed flyscreen on the museum door clicked shut behind her. She slipped a cold glass of champagne into Meg's hand.

Meg smiled. "What's this for?"

"Primer." Aunty Phyl sat down on the bench beside her. "I see heartache coming. Well, not me because I don't have the gift, but rather Edwina does."

Meg lifted the glass and took a sip, letting the tart fizz rest on her tongue until the bubbles dissipated before swallowing. If Jack wanted to leave, she wouldn't stop him, but she would leave the door open if he wanted to return. Granny Mary had always said that love was like a carrier pigeon. You set it free and if it returned to you, it was yours forever.

Phyl eyed her over the rim of her reading glasses. "You love him."

"With all my heart."

"Yes, you have that glow about you." She sighed, a long drawn out breath that came from deep inside. "Meg, darling, sometimes I think we've held you back, Mary and I."

"That's not true." She leaned her head against Phyl's shoulder, her nose twitching at the mixed scent of lavender, lemon and eucalyptus mothballs that still clung stubbornly to the material of her aunt's dress. "I'm right where I want to be."

"Are you, darling girl?"

"Yes." She could say that with all the conviction of honesty in her heart. "I love this museum as much as Granny did. It's a part of me and I can't imagine not having it — or you — in my life."

"I'm not going to be around forever, sweet. My number will be up one day too." Phyl's head came to rest against hers, her ringed fingers tracing the droplets of condensation on the crystal champagne flute.

"I'll still have the memories when you're gone." Neither her aunt nor her granny had ever sugar-coated anything in life.

"And what if, after all this, we don't get that damned grant?"

"Then I'll go to Plan B."

She watched Jack shake hands with Rob and Lyn, wrapping up the interview. If she had to canvass every bank and loan company nationwide, she'd find the funding somehow. Even if it meant putting up the house as collateral, but she wouldn't let the museum die without exploring all avenues. With the Sullivans expanding their farming and buying up more land, she'd have a good chance at getting extra seasonal work to cover loan repayments.

"We can diversify. Find something we don't have in Bindarra Creek yet and add that to our repertoire. Maybe we can do re-enactments or theatre productions out in the sorting shed. I'll come up with something."

"And what about Jack?" Phyl lifted her head.

What about Jack? Could a long distance relationship work? She loved waking up to him in the morning, his warm, hard body close, her head pillowed against his shoulder and the feel of his skin under her hands. She could only answer honestly. "I don't know, Aunty Phyl."

Riley pulled up in the patrol car with Nobby in the passenger seat beside him. Meg's heart flipped. Surely though, if the police were going to lay charges, Nobby would be cuffed in the back, not the front? She sat up as Aunty Phyl tensed beside her.

Riley got out and opened the door for Nobby, helping him out of the car. "Look who I ran into checking himself out of hospital."

Meg stood and rushed over to take Nobby's other arm for balance as the old man took a moment to find his feet.

"Stubborn old bastard," said Aunty Phyl. "Why didn't you call us to come and get you?"

"A g'day and a welcome home whiskey would be nice," Nobby grumbled as he hooked a carry bag with the hospital dispensary logo on it over his wrist.

"You can't drink. You're on antibiotics." Aunty Phyl held out her hand for the carry bag. "I'll take care of those for you."

Nobby turned to Riley. "See? Nagged at the hospital, nagged at home. Told you a cell at the station would be quieter."

Riley chuckled, stepping back as Aunty Phyl

slipped in to replace him at Nobby's side. "Not so sure about that with young AJ around. I'll get your bag out of the boot. Meg, the doc says she'll give you a ring later about Nobby's care over the next few weeks."

"Thanks, Riley." Meg kissed Nobby's leathery cheek. "Welcome home. Come and have a seat, take a minute to get your breath back."

They eased him onto the bench. He eyed champagne flutes next to him longingly. Aunty Phyl caught him looking and scooped them up to take them away. "Don't even think about it. I'll bring you a glass of water."

Nobby grinned. "Worth a try. A cuppa would be nice, Phyl."

"Nobby!" Yells rose from down the street as the Lawson kids pounded down the pavement from the direction of the hospital, led by the eldest boy, Scotty. They crowded in around the bench, all ten of them talking at once, each with a gift in their hands.

Riley carried Nobby's bag inside and came back out with a soft drink in his hand. "Cheers, thanks, Ms Moonie," he called out to Aunty Phyl and patted Meg's shoulder as he passed her on his way to the wagon. "See you later, Meg. Give me a shout if you need anything. Like crowd control." He grinned as the kids argued over who got to sit next to Nobby on the bench.

"Thanks for bringing him home, Riley. And for everything."

"You can thank me when the coroner's report is

released. But, off the record, it was an accidental death, Meg. There was no criminal intent present at all. No charges will be laid."

Relief flooded her. Grief and regret would always be with them, but now was a time for healing. She waved to Riley as he drove away with a blip of the siren and a flash of the red and blue lights for the kids' entertainment.

As the patrol car disappeared down toward Gilles Bridge, Jack said goodbye to the Stones and crossed the road.

He'd seen that tender moment between Meg and Phyllis when their heads had been close together, deep in conversation, champagne glasses catching the glint of the sun. And Bennie had caught the moment Nobby had arrived home on camera. All their footage so far today had captured many special moments on the streets of Bindarra Creek.

Pleased with the day's work, he'd looked forward to a quiet night alone with Meg. Those nights were too few and too precious to miss as he neared the end of his time in Bindarra Creek. But with Nobby home, it looked like it was going to be an evening of celebration instead.

Jack scoffed at his thoughts. Only a few short weeks ago he'd strolled into town, counting the hours until he could leave again. How things had changed. If he hadn't been given a deadline for submission of the material, he would have dragged out the filming so they could stay a little longer.

He stopped in front of Meg. "Hey."

Her smile lit up her eyes. "Hey. Good day at the office?"

"You could say that." He wanted to kiss her but Phyllis made him nervous as she stared at him over those bright pink reading glasses from behind the park bench. "That was the last of the interviews."

Her smile slipped a little. "That's good, right?"

Jack shrugged. If he remained non-committal, he wouldn't have to think about the weeks and months ahead. "I see Nobby's home."

He gave the man a wave. Nobby sat on the bench, surrounded by children, going through each of his gifts one by one — everything from a bag of lollies to a sad-looking cactus in need of some love.

"Yes. We're going to let him have a rest this afternoon and then, once I've cleared it with the doc, we'll take him down to the Riverside Pub for dinner. Will you come too?" Her fingers slipped through his, drawing their hands between them.

"I wouldn't miss it for the world." Jack lifted her hands to kiss her knuckles. He wanted to ask her to stay the night with him, but that would be selfish on Nobby's first night home.

"We might need your help with Nobby tonight.

And he might appreciate some male assistance." She stepped in closer, her voice low and sexy. "Would you like to stay over?"

His heart swelled just a little. "I think that would be a great idea."

Her green gaze met his. "Thank you, Jack."

"He can sleep on the couch," called Phyllis. "And no sneaking around in the middle of the night."

Jack groaned. "Does she have supersonic hearing?"

A soft laugh escaped Meg. "It's her superpower."

He focused on the words as they slipped from her lips. Powerless to resist, he placed a brief kiss on her mouth.

Nobby chuckled. "Looks like you might need earplugs tonight, Phyllis."

The chuckle brought on a coughing spasm. Meg stepped away and turned toward the museum, her hand still wrapped in Jack's. "Come on, Nobby. Let's get you inside." She ushered all the kids together. "Come back tomorrow, guys. Nobby will be feeling a bit stronger after a rest."

"Thanks for the presents," the old man called as the children began to disperse.

Jack picked up Nobby's bag off the pavement and held out his hand to help him up. Meg supported him from the other side, and together they walked him through the gate, into the house adjacent to the museum, with Phyllis leading the way.

While the two ladies went to put the kettle on for a

cup of tea, Jack helped Nobby settle into the room he'd once shared with Mary. Weary and weakened by his illness, the old man sat on the edge of the bed, breathing heavily. He reached out for the framed photograph of a much younger Mary, running his fingers over the glass as Jack stowed the bag near an antique wardrobe.

"She was beautiful, my Mary. Always so patient, kind and understanding." He dashed away a tear that slipped down his cheek. "So proud and independent, and so very bloody stubborn. A treasure worth more than the gold buried in the hills."

"I wish I'd had the chance to meet her." Jack moved to sit beside Nobby.

"This photo was taken before she met Carrick." He handed it to Jack. "It broke my heart when she fell for him. But I was a young stockman with itchy feet and an aversion to putting down roots, so I left the way open for him to sweep her off her feet. Silly me."

Jack studied the faded colour image in the photograph. Taken somewhere in the late fifties, perhaps early sixties, Mary's resemblance to Meg was uncanny. "She was beautiful."

"Yes, she was. I see a lot of her in young Meg. The problem with love, son, is that sometimes we don't know what we have until it's gone. And then it's too late. With Mary, I always had something good to look forward to coming home to. No matter where my feet led me." Nobby kicked off his running shoes, exposing a hole in his sock. He wiggled his toes. "I miss that damn woman so much. And I'll never forgive myself for not labelling those teas. Hopefully, when we meet again, she'll forgive me."

Jack patted Nobby's shoulder then placed the photograph back on the nightstand. "I'm sure she will." He reached inside the collar of his polo shirt and slipped his press lanyard over his head, then released the moonstone ring from the clip. "I kept the ring safe for you." He dropped it into Nobby's outstretched palm.

The old man's fingers curled around it, pressing it deep into his hand. For a moment, he closed his eyes, his breathing shallow. When he opened them again, he tucked the ring into the top pocket of Jack's polo shirt. "Hang onto it until the time is right. If you still choose to leave when you're done, I'll take it back and keep it safe for when the right man for Meg comes along."

A stab of jealousy coloured Jack's world green. The thought of another man sweeping Meg off her feet the way Carrick had stolen Mary from under Nobby's nose made his gut curl.

"How did you know Mary was the one for you?" Jack stood to pace the worn and scarred jarrah floorboards.

With a sigh, Nobby stretched out on the bed, his eyes on the pressed, patterned ceiling. "The minute I realised I was too late. She walked into the Valentine's Ball on Carrick's arm, a beautiful outback princess in a blue swirly dress, all starry-eyed and glowing. Carrick was a handsome devil, full of Irish charm and wit. What chance did a sunburnt stockman have against a gentleman of the world?"

"Did she know you loved her?"

Nobby smiled. "No. It was a different time back then. Carrick could offer her a life of comfort I couldn't, so I never told Mary how I felt about her until he'd left her with a mountain of debt and a baby to raise alone." He sighed. "She didn't love me right away, but she trusted me. Mary was a damn proud woman. She wouldn't accept any financial help from me, but we went from friends to lovers over the years. I don't regret a minute of the time we spent together. Only the time we spent apart."

Jack tried to think about how he'd feel walking away from Bindarra Creek. How he'd feel about leaving Meg behind to find someone else. It didn't sit well on his mind. But was he Carrick or Nobby? Would the bright lights, hustle and bustle, and the excitement of his job lure him back to the city streets or could he be like ex-investment broker Dan Molyneaux and settle for a tree-change?

Meg walked into the room, Phyllis behind her with a tray of tea and biscuits. Jack moved to clear a space on the nightstand for Nobby's tea. He had less than a week to work it out.

CHAPTER FIFTEEN

*E*xcitement buzzed as everyone squeezed into the pub. Dan had put another television up on the wall so no one missed out. They'd put on extra wait staff so no one had to wait too long for a drink and Maureen had outdone herself with the plates of nibbles doing the rounds. Cheers went up as the program came on air.

Bindarra Creek — A Town Reborn. The title flashed up behind Kelsey O'Donnell's shoulder as she read out the introduction from the plush studio in Sydney. There was still time for drinks and gossip because their story held second slot in the segments. Nerves set the butterflies churning in Meg's tummy.

"It'll be good, you'll see." Jack's warmth filled her space.

"I'm sure you've done us proud, thank you."

Jack's gaze held hers. "It's been my pleasure."

Meg reached up to straighten his collar. "It's been great having you here. We'll miss you." A band of sadness squeezed at her chest. She'd always known he'd go back to the city. A town like Bindarra Creek couldn't hold onto a guy like Jack.

He reached up to capture her hands, held them against the beat of his heart. "You could come with me, Meg."

"What would I do in the city? My life is here. Yours is out there in the big wide world, wherever your next story takes you."

The words came out on a tight note, her throat closing around them. What would she do alone in a city apartment, waiting for him to return? No matter how much she loved him, she couldn't live like that. The people of Bindarra Creek were her life blood, the museum, her heart. Everything she was, was right here in this town. And Jack, as sweet and hot as his kisses were, had never promised forever because he didn't believe in love.

"I'll always be right here, Jack." Meg reached up on tiptoes to press a kiss to his mouth, a soft sweep of his lips with a taste of goodbye.

He released her hands to put his arms around her and drew her close. He kissed her back with an intensity and gentleness that tasted of reluctance to leave. Hope flared a little brighter that perhaps Jack had found the place he wanted to put down roots.

A cheer went up around them as the television host

cut to their story. Jack released Meg from his hold as she got swept up in the crowd.

Alice hooked her arm through Meg's. "Come on, hon, you should have a VIP seat for this. I've saved one up the front for you."

She looked around for Jack. This was his moment too. He should be there beside her, but he'd been surrounded by people, patting his back, shaking his hand before the program had even aired. Excitement crackled in the air. Bindarra Creek was about to have its five minutes of fame.

The camera cut to Jack's face on the screen as he made the introductions. It followed him as he strolled up Main Street, picked out Edwina on a bench, sneaking a smoke. Cut to Nobby, all bandaged up, being transferred from the ambulance outside the newly upgraded Bindarra Creek Hospital. Focused on the shabby front of the museum and Phyllis with a glass of whiskey in one hand and a cigar in the other.

Mary's cellar haven had been portrayed as the den of a witch who dabbled in black magic rather than a woman who'd held the heart and history of her town in her hands.

Jack's commentary and his interview with Meg had all the good bits edited out, leaving only the impression of a dying town rather than one they'd worked hard to rebuild. The community spirit had been chopped right out of the story.

Tears rolled down Meg's cheeks as the last of her

dream to save the museum was hacked to pieces as the words that came out of Jack's mouth labelled it, "A run-down shack not worth saving."

Silence fell faster than a stone in the creek as shock registered on the faces of the crowd squeezed into the pub.

Devastated, Meg turned to look at Jack. He stood near the door with his hands clenched at his sides, his spine ramrod straight and his eyes glued to the screen, his face devoid of expression. She willed him to say something, anything. An apology, a denial, an excuse. But his lips never moved as he turned and walked away.

Meg pushed through the crowd and followed him out into the night. "Jack!"

He stopped, hand in his pockets, shoulders stiff.

"What ...? What the hell was that?" Shock raised goosebumps on her arms, chilled her blood.

"That was ratings reporting."

"Is that what you call it?" Hurt suppressed the anger that simmered under the surface of her question. She'd been at those shoots, and the script that had come on screen was not the one he'd shot. Meg tried for calm. "I'd call it false reporting."

"I don't do the edits, Meg." His voice was quiet in the night as he stood with his back to her.

"And you didn't view the segment after the editing had been done?"

Jack shook his head. "Out of my control. I research, I report, end of story."

Meg turned as the door of the pub opened and people spilled out into the car park, voices raised in anger and disbelief.

Bennie got pushed out from the crowd and sent packing by Old Man Jake. "And don't you come back into this pub again, young man."

"There are a lot of angry, disappointed people back there, Jack. They deserve an explanation." Damn it, she deserved one too. He'd stolen her kisses, ripped out her heart and stomped on it with his final cut of coverage for the story.

Jack turned his head a little, but not enough to look her in the eyes. "I don't have an explanation."

Meg walked toward him, her legs shaking. With a hand on his arm, she turned him around, her eyes searching his face. "Then find me one. I have to go into damage control, Jack. I'm the one who brought you here. I'm the one who has to fix this."

The ache of disappointment and shattered dreams clung to her throat. She'd brought the town and its people into disrepute trying to keep Mary's dream alive.

Everything she'd feared the station would do had come true. They'd made her town the laughingstock in a program that would have viewers taking the mickey out of them from the comfort of their city couches, never knowing the real story of a struggling small town reborn.

"Jack ..." Her voice cracked on his name, emotion swarming up from beneath her ribs and swamping her.

Anger radiated off him in waves, his mouth pulled tight, his gaze flashing to hers. "I'll deal with it." Her hand slipped off his arm as he walked away in long, angry strides.

Seconds later, Aunty Phyllis filled the space he'd vacated. "Let him go, Meg. He's a no good, double-crossing, son-of-a—"

"Stop, Phyl." Meg held her hand up, the shards of her heart piercing her lungs and stealing her breath.

"Well, I'm just saying—"

Meg threw an arm around her aunt's shoulders and hugged her. "I know what you're saying and I know you mean well. We'll be fine. I know we will. We can rebuild without that grant. Somehow, I'll make it work."

"Will you, Meg? Because, this time, I believe you really loved that scumbag."

Meg leaned her head against her aunt's. "I really do."

She'd trusted another man exactly like Logan. And just like that two-timing low-life, Jack Hughes had broken her heart and walked away.

CHAPTER SIXTEEN

*F*riday morning dawned bright and sunny, a total contrast to his black mood. After yet another fruitless attempt at trying to speak to anyone at the station, Jack threw his clothes into his suitcase, not caring if he crumpled his expensive business shirts. No one would take his calls. God damn it, when he got back to Sydney, someone in production and further up the ladder had better have some bloody answers ready for him.

He rubbed a hand over his chin, feeling the rasp of two days' growth. If Meg had been mad at him, yelled at him — God damn it, even punched him in the nose — he'd have felt better.

Instead, she'd looked at him with disappointment and her heart in her eyes, her devastation stealing his breath with a blow to the solar plexus, making him feel one hundred percent the total shit he was. He rubbed at the ache in his chest. He hadn't planned on falling in love. With Meg. With the people of Bindarra Creek.

He'd spent the past two days exiled to a corner of the Riverside Pub, the recipient of stabbing glares and cold shoulders. With the exception of Dan's mum, Maureen, who'd continued to bring him hot plates of food. And Dan, who'd supplied beer on tap — on the house — and a shoulder pat or two as Jack had drowned his sorrows and guilty conscience. Until even that avenue of escape had been taken from him when Curly the Cockatoo had shat in his beer glass. A nice big green runny poop that had marred the pristine white of the foam head, dead in the centre. The ultimate fuck-you-Jack-Hughes.

Jeremy Forster had returned Betty intact, with a new radiator and — thankfully — no damage to the engine. At the very least, he had a reliable getaway car. Jack had half-expected to find another message carved into her paintwork by a lynch mob. Instead, Jeremy had brought her back looking as good as new with a perfectly colour-matched, repaired fender. But then the man knew what it was like to be an outsider.

The organisers of tonight's Valentine's Ball had withdrawn his invitation, hence there'd been no reason to shave nor any need for the freshly-pressed white shirt and black dress pants. There was nothing to keep him in town now that the story had aired and the hopes of the people had been dashed that it would bring thousands of tourists to town. He wished he'd told his boss to stick this assignment right up his arse.

Jack's phone buzzed with an incoming call. Speak of the devil. He didn't even try to keep the bark from his voice as he answered, "I'm done. I quit."

"Oh, come on, Jack." Darren's tone mocked him from the other end of the call. "The segment has got people laughing all over Australia."

"At the expense of the people in this town. That wasn't the object of the story." All the good bits had ended up on the editing floor and the content stripped until the heart of the story had been ripped out and stomped on.

"It's a small town, Jack. Already forgotten. No one was ever going to rush over there and make the town famous by turning their plight into a movie. Who cares?"

Jack slammed the lid of his suitcase closed, bitter anger rushing through him. "I do."

The story he'd wanted to portray and the one that had come through had been poles apart. He'd wanted success for Bindarra Creek and the museum, happiness for Meg and Aunty Phyl. Instead he'd destroyed Meg's last hope of getting a grant and the town was now a ball of string the fat cats would toy with for amusement. Any minute now, that lynch mob would be knocking on his door to see him out of town.

Darren's snort of laughter made Jack want to wrap his hands around the arrogant bastard's neck and squeeze. "Getting soft in your old age, Hughes? What happened to my hard-nosed correspondent? The man who walked into war zones, who took on the cheats in parliament? Tamryn Hollister and her father have withdrawn all allegations against you. Hollister himself will be making a public apology to you shortly. You're all set for your next big assignment, Jack. We're sending you to Hong Kong to cover the unrest there."

Jack walked over to the window and pushed the curtain aside. Down in the car park, Meg stood talking to Alice. She glanced up at him and their eyes met. God, she was beautiful. And he'd broken her heart with his portrayal of the town. No, not him. Darren and his damn petty ratings war.

Meg looked away, turned her back on him. He swallowed the pain of rejection. He deserved it, and if he wanted to win her back along with the hearts of the townsfolk, he'd need a damn good plan.

An idea niggled in his mind. Could he pull it off? He could, if the production team were on his side. But he'd need someone on the inside too. Jack grinned as Edwina's voice whispered through his mind. *Choices, Jack Hughes. Choices.*

"Jack? I thought you'd be excited that we're air-lifting you out of Shit Creek."

Below, Alice pulled Meg into a hug. His own eyes stung as Jack realised Meg was crying. He'd never meant to hurt her. "How about 'fuck you', Darren?"

He hung up and tossed his phone onto the bed,

then went to knock on Bennie's room door. There'd be favours to call in, arms to be twisted, rules to be broken, but he'd fix this if it was the last assignment he ever got as a correspondent for the program and for any news channel again.

Several hours of knee-crawling and genuine, heartfelt butt-kissing later, his lips were dry and his throat ached from begging. He'd practically surrendered naming rights for his first child to Aunty Phyllis in return for her support — if Meg didn't chop off his balls first, her words not his — and he owed the entire production team and a few key people at the station a decade-worth of drinks at the Riverside Pub. And if he ever met the chairperson of the Royal Australian Historical Society in person, he'd kiss her and buy her that gin and tonic.

Now all he had to do was pull off the plan and not get lynched by the CWA or the Valentine's Ball planning committee, who were pretty much one and the same.

Jack shaved the stubble from his face, graciously accepted his freshly re-pressed shirt and trousers from Maureen and dressed for the Valentine's Ball.

He straightened his bow tie and grinned at himself in the mirror. *Take that, James Bond.* Tonight it would take every ounce of charm in his arsenal to fix what had been broken. Excitement unlike anything he'd known before coursed through his blood, expectation driving his hopes to dizzying heights.

Jack reached for the suit jacket. For the first time in his life, he wanted this more than anything his career could offer. He checked his watch. Six forty-five. The ball started at seven. Bang on time.

A knock before the door opened, and Bennie poked his head around it. "Ready?"

"Ready as I'll ever be."

Bennie grinned, his face flushed with excitement. "You know the shit will hit the fan at the station, right?"

Jack couldn't wait. "As long as your job is safe. You're a good cameraman, Bennie. I wouldn't want to see you get fired over this."

"All good, mate. Your ex has it covered. She's gone into bat for us now that your name has been cleared in that viral video saga."

A flush warmed Jack through. When he'd called Kelsey to cash in on that favour she'd promised, she'd been all in for the challenge. *I'm glad you found someone to love, Jack.* She'd wished him well and promised her support in his plan to win Meg's heart.

"Right, let's go." Jack swallowed the nerves fluttering in his gut and wished he had a whiskey to calm them.

He followed Bennie and the camera equipment down the stairs into the pub where Old Man Jake and

Granddad Charlie waited to sneak them into the town hall through a side entrance.

Outside, stars danced in the sky and the night sounds of the bush came to life around them. A rush of pride and affection for the place he'd come to love took Jack by surprise. How had he ever thought Bindarra Creek was a shithole? It lived and breathed with the spirit of the outback, where people bickered and feuded, yet when the going got tough, they all pulled together. He wanted to be a part of that.

They bundled themselves and the gear into Dan's new four-wheel drive SUV, given with his permission. Bennie solved the argument of who would drive because, between Charlie and Old Man Jake, a debate could go on all night. As they inched toward the hall with Old Man Jake at the wheel, Jack wished Bennie had driven instead. At this rate, the ball would be over before they got there. Panic replaced the nerves.

"Want me to drive?" Jack offered.

"Nope."

Curly reaffirmed the refusal with a flap of his wings and a battle cry from his beak. Clearly the bird still hadn't forgiven him. An excruciating number of minutes later, Old Man Jake cut the headlights and they pulled up quietly behind the hall. Laughter mixed with voices raised above the music coming from inside.

Old Man Jake eased out from behind the wheel, his joints stiff from the short drive which didn't put a damper on his excitement to be involved in a covert operation. He armed himself with his toy gun that shot foam pellets.

"What do you need that for, you old fool," Granddad Charlie asked.

"In case they don't shut up and listen. Everyone will be quacking like ducks in there when this boy walks in. Next thing you know they'll be roping him in like a randy bull and sending him off to the slaughterhouse before he can say boo."

Jack shivered. "Thanks, mate. Glad you've got my back."

"Gotta look after a bloke. Open the door, Charlie."

Bennie hooked his equipment bag onto his back and picked up the camera out of the four-wheel drive. "Ready, Jack?" He checked his watch. "We're scheduled to cut into the program at exactly seven pm. Kelsey will transition it. I'll start filming as soon as you enter the hall."

Jack blew out a nervous breath and shook out his hands to get the circulation flowing again. He hadn't been this nervous since his first assignment as a freshly pressed correspondent. "Let's do it." Before his balls shrivelled and he lost his nerve.

"Wait for the cue." Jake held up his hand.

The music died as Florrie Miller called for everyone's attention. She launched into her welcome speech and took care of the housekeeping rules for the night before saying, "We have a surprise lined up before the ball gets into full swing and we can enjoy ourselves."

Bennie pressed a microphone into Jack's hand then counted down, whispering, "In five … four … three … two … one!"

Charlie held the door open as Jack walked through it, his knees knocking with nerves. From a chair near the stage, Nobby gave him the thumbs up. *Make sure you've got that ring on you, boy.* The freshly unveiled television on stage showed Kelsey cueing them in.

"And now, we cross live to Bindarra Creek to join our favourite correspondent, Jack Hughes, on location at the annual Valentine's Ball. Over to you, Jack."

Florrie turned down the sound on the television as arranged. He could only imagine the chaos Kelsey would be dealing with as the camera cut to him. Jack swallowed the lump in his throat.

"Thank you, Kelsey. Folks, a few days ago we went to air with the story of a struggling town. Unfortunately, we didn't do Bindarra Creek or its people justice in that story. Stories are meant to be unbiased, to explore and report facts. What they're not meant to do is take the piss out of a town that has worked incredibly hard to rebuild everything they've lost."

He walked further into the hall. The crowd melted back, clearing a path to the front stage as Bennie walked backwards with the camera on his shoulder, keeping Jack front and centre.

Up front, next to Aunty Phyllis, stood Meg. A vision in a soft, floaty, blue vintage dress that showcased her creamy skin, her chin lifted with a stubborn set to her jaw he hoped to have the opportunity to kiss away later. Her blonde hair was twisted into a style from probably the forties or something. How would he know? He was just a guy. It didn't matter. She was beautiful with the tumble of curls over her shoulder, secured with some kind of clip that sparkled under the lights.

"The story I wanted to tell was one of courage, commitment and dedication." Jack held Meg's gaze as he walked toward her, his heart pounding in his chest and doubt thundering through his mind. What if she told him to get lost? "The story of a woman saving a dream and her heritage."

Her lips parted as he stopped beside her, all glossy and inviting. Jack took her hand and lifted it to his lips, pressing a soft kiss to her fingertips.

"I'm sorry I missed the mark." He kept his hand curled around hers as he faced the crowd. "I came to cover a story on a dying town steeped in hardship and instead what I found was the seedlings of new life in a community that stood together to achieve their goal. I found a landscape rich in character, and our initial program failed to capture the essence of that character. So, tonight, I'm going to tell you what this town really means to me, a man hardened by reality and the anonymity of city life."

Jack walked to the centre of the dance floor, Meg beside him. "Life began for me the day I walked into a dusty museum in a small town called Bindarra Creek. A town full of country pride and the spirit of determination. As an outsider, a stranger, an unknown entity, I was welcomed with open arms, given access to the deepest, darkest secrets and invited to share in the celebrations of success. Not once did anyone question my integrity. Well, except for Aunty Phyllis." He turned to give her a smile as the crowd chuckled. "I betrayed that trust by following the rules. Tonight I'm breaking them so I can set a few facts straight. This is a town full of character, warmth and hospitality. It's a town that deserves to survive. A community where strength and struggle go hand in hand, yet nothing can kill the spirit that abounds here. From divine baklava to foul-mouthed cockatoos, and amid all the wonderful, colourful characters who live here, there is no place I'd rather be."

Jack placed an arm around Meg's shoulders, hugged her closer and looked into her eyes. She looked back at him, her gaze full of uncertainty. "As someone wise once told me, Bindarra Creek isn't just any small town. It's a living, breathing, beating heart." He looked back at the camera. "This is Jack Hughes, signing out, for the last time, from Bindarra Creek. A town — and a man — reborn."

Bennie reached out for the mike, the camera still balanced on his shoulder. Jack turned to face Meg as the music came on and the lights in the hall dimmed. Frankie Blue Eyes crooned about the way she looked tonight.

"May I have this dance?" He held out his hand.

Meg placed her shaking hand in his as he let his arm drop from her shoulders to her waist and held her close. They moved in time to the music, their bodies brushing, their voices silent until the song changed.

Jack brushed his lips against her temple. "I'm sorry, Meg. I never meant to hurt you. Or anyone else."

She nodded. "You'll be in trouble with the station."

"I quit my job."

Meg pulled back to look at him. "Jack, why? You're crazy."

"Am I? Am I crazy for being hopelessly in love with you, Meg? For wanting to stay right here in Bindarra Creek and take on the responsibility of that crazy museum with you, if you'll let me?"

"Jack ..." Her whisper brushed his lips as she stopped dancing.

"I'm not Carrick Kenny or Logan McGee. I don't gamble, I'm financially stable, I don't have a wife tucked away, and I have a promise from the state's security office that assures me I won't be having any more trouble from that viral video." He placed both hands on her hips and anchored her close. "Please let me stay and love you."

Vaguely aware that the music had died amid the hush that had fallen on the hall, Jack released his hold on Meg to go down on one knee, praying she'd give him the answer he wanted so desperately to hear. He reached into his pocket and pulled out a small red velvet pouch. From inside it, he drew out the moonstone ring Nobby had given him.

"Nobby gave Mary this ring when he promised to be faithful to her for the rest of their lifetime. She wanted you to have it when you found the man you wanted to spend forever with." Pocketing the velvet pouch, Jack reached for her hand with his heart pounding in his throat. "I'd like nothing more than to be that man. Please spend a lifetime with me."

"Jack, please ... stand up. You've done enough."

His heart stalled and sank. Slowly he stood. Was she going to turn him down, feed him to the lynch mob, kick his sorry arse out of town? He'd given his last chance all he had. "Members of the board at The Royal Australian Historical Society will be arriving in town next week to assess and discuss your grant proposal. They're interested, Meg. It's the very least I could do to make it up to you."

"Oh, Jack. What happened wasn't your fault, but you tried to fix it. You could have left town and not done anything about it, but you didn't. You stayed. That's enough. Did you mean what you said about spending a lifetime with me? Here in Bindarra Creek?"

"Every word." That much he knew without any doubt in his mind. "I love you, Meg Moonie, and I want to promise you forever. We can travel if you like. I'll show you the world, but we'll always come home to Bindarra Creek."

She reached her arms up to place them over his shoulders, her hands drawing his forehead to hers. "Say it again, Jack."

"I love you, Meg Moonie. You, your crazy Aunty Phyllis — who has it written in blood that she gets to name our first child — and everyone else in this town. For the first time in my life, I feel like I belong in a place where I can put down roots and stay forever."

"I want to believe you. About everything you've said tonight. How do I know you mean it?"

"Let me show you."

Jack's mouth found Meg's. He kissed her with every ounce of the love in his heart, every essence of his soul, putting into actions what words failed to deliver. And when she kissed him back, he knew without a doubt that she'd promised him forever.

As the music began to play again and the buzz of conversation resumed, he heard Bennie call, "And that's a wrap, folks."

The End

Note from the Author

Thank you so much for taking the time to read *Promise Me Forever* which is part of the group writing venture, *Bindarra Creek - A Town Reborn* series.

If you would like to know more about upcoming releases or would love to talk anything book related, please join my street team at Book Love with Juanita Kees or sign up for my quarterly newsletter. I'd love your company.

If you've enjoyed your journey to Bindarra Creek today, please leave a review. All reviews are appreciated.

Read on for an excerpt from *Home to Bindarra Creek* (A Bindarra Creek Romance, series 1).

Juanita Kees

EXCERPT - HOME TO BINDARRA CREEK

BY JUANITA KEES

A BINDARRA CREEK ROMANCE

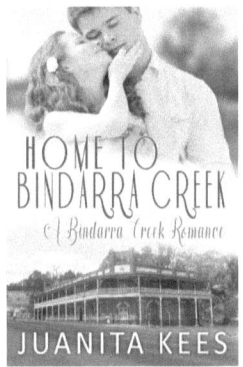

CHAPTER ONE

*D*an Molyneaux eased his V8 sedan around the bend and into the straight with the effortlessness of an experienced driver who enjoyed the power in his hands and the roar of the engine under the hood.

Out here in the country with no traffic on the road for miles, he could push it to the speed limit and blow the cobwebs from the pistons. Just the way he liked it. If only it was as easy to erase the guilt from his heart.

He accelerated up the hill to the rise ahead, preparing for the drop that would lie beyond. His heart pumped hard with adrenaline in anticipation of the downward slope to come. The g-force would drag at his abs and suck the breath from his lungs on a *Yes!*

For the first time in months, he was free. Unchained from a desk job that had destroyed his faith in humanity and a million-dollar view that was no compensation for his mistakes.

The downhill came and didn't disappoint, but as the road stretched out in front of him and momentum carried him towards the next bend, a kangaroo burst from the bush onto the road. He braked—hard and fast —the red alert flashing on his screen display, warning him of the impending impact. He knew if he swerved to avoid the animal, he'd roll the car or hit a tree or worse, kill himself.

The rear end fishtailed and as he struggled to control the skid, the front end collided with the roo and rolled it onto the hood. The impact of its head against the glass sent cracks running across the windscreen.

"Fuck!"

He steered into the curve of the road as he stepped harder on the brakes, the stench of burning rubber in his nostrils, and felt the drag of the automatic braking system as it slowed the travel. The car rolled to a stop in the ditch and the cabin filled with the burning smell of death.

Dan's hands shook on the wheel. His heart pumped hard in his chest, and even though he knew there was nothing he could have done to avoid hitting the roo, guilt rushed at him. More blood on his hands.

"Damn it!"

For a moment he sat gathering his wits, calming his pulse, mentally calculating his speed at point of impact. Even though he hadn't been over the speed limit, the emergency braking system would only have shaved off a quarter of the speed before the car hit. Eighty kilometres per hour. If thc roo was alive, it would be pretty beat up. Not the animal's lucky day and certainly not his either.

His heart still pounding, he stared at the roo lying prone on the hood, its snout only inches from his own nose. Only centimetres and a wrecked sheet of glass had stood between him and death or at the very least, serious injury.

Once again, he stared death in the face. The glassy eyes of the roo staring back at him brought back visions of another death where the sightless eyes were human.

He pushed open the car door, the metallic squawk from the hinges warning him of the damage to expect. With a wary eye on the roo, he stepped out onto the bitumen where thick tracks of rubber layered the road, evidence of his close shave. Keeping his distance, he examined the wreck.

Spidery veins spread around the hole in the windscreen, the only thing maintaining the concave shape and stopping it from collapsing was the shatterproof film. The hood wore the indent of the kangaroo's body pressed into the metal, and the front end formed a perfect vee.

Dan wasn't sure who was worse off, the car or the kangaroo. The car could be fixed but he thought it might be too late for the roo.

He checked his phone. Thank God he had a signal.

It meant he wasn't in the middle of nowhere, miles away from civilisation.

Who to call? Mum first, because she was expecting him. She'd be worried if he didn't show up on time. Plus, after almost twelve months in the backwater town of Bindarra Creek, she'd know who to call for a tow.

Next, he'd call the insurance company. He pressed out his mother's number and waited for her to answer.

"Dan! Where are you?"

"Hey, Mum. Don't panic, I'm okay. I had a little accident." He raked a still shaky hand through his hair. "I hit a roo."

The familiar sound of her voice eased over the shock, reminding him of his childhood—when it was just the two of them, when she'd encouraged him to spread his wings and been there to patch up his wounds when he'd fallen. Warmth flooded his heart, filling a little of the void that plagued him. He should have made an effort to see her before now.

He clenched his jaw. There'd been nothing stopping him from making the trip sooner except he'd been too busy ruining people's lives with investments doomed to fail. Perhaps that's why he hadn't thought twice about investing in a rundown pub in a nowhere town—penance for his sins.

If he failed, he'd be kissing a couple of hundred thousand of his invested dollars goodbye. He hoped to God that hitting the roo wasn't another sign of Karma having a field day with his life.

"Oh Dan, honey. Are you okay? Where?"

Dan looked around for a signpost, anything that might give him a clue. "About forty k's from Bindarra Creek."

"Oh, honey! Not a good way to start your new life, is it?"

He scratched his head then pressed his fingertips to his gritty eyes. "No, it isn't." God, he must be close to burnout if his eyes stung more for the dead kangaroo than they did for his equally dead V8.

"Hang in there, Dan. I'll give our local mechanic a call to come down and tow you in."

"I can call it in, Mum. Give me his number. I'll have to give him my insurance details anyway." He lifted his head at the sound of an engine gearing down and the swish of tyres on gravel. The yellow rotating lights flashed on the light bar of the white four-wheel drive ute, illuminating the signwriting on the hood—Bindarra Creek National Park Ranger. "Looks like help in some form has arrived. The ranger just pulled up."

His mum chuckled. "That'll be Alice. She'll take care of you and the roo. Leave the rest to me. It's not like you're going to do a runner on old Fred. He can get all the nitty-gritty details from you later. Besides, you're going to have your hands full in a minute, filling out Alice's environmental accident reports."

"Great! And here I was thinking I was done with paperwork. Thanks, Mum," he said and pressed the end call button. *Alice?* The name echoed in his head, but the shock of the accident had clouded his mind and he pushed aside the niggling feeling he should know the name.

Hand on the buckled roof frame of his car, Dan watched as the ranger got out of the ute and walked toward him, the butt of her rifle balanced against her shoulder, the barrel pointed to the ground.

The thunderous expression on her face and the grim, tight line of her lips had him praying the rifle was meant for the roo and not for him. She stopped a few feet in front of him and eyed the damage to the car. Without a word, she brushed past him and headed for the kangaroo. Rifle ready, she aimed for the head.

Dan's heart lurched in his throat. "You're going to shoot it?"

She threw him a black look over her shoulder. "It's the quickest way to put her out of her misery. It's what we have to do when motorists wipe them out."

The way she said *motorist* twisted his gut. The disdain, the hatred, the hurt. No, the feisty ranger wasn't enjoying this any more than he was. "I'm sorry. It was just there. I could never have stopped in time without hitting a tree and killing myself. It's dead."

Dan caught a look at her paling features as she turned away and aimed again. Her words were unsteady when she spoke. "Roos are clever at playing dead. It's their safety mechanism. No matter how bad their injuries are they run on adrenalin—just like humans. If their legs are broken, they'll still get up, kick the shit out of you and run away, only to die from shock and injuries somewhere in the bush."

She approached the roo cautiously, rifle ready. The roo lifted its head, brown eyes round and wide. It struggled to lift the weight of its body, rolled off the hood, shuddered and fell onto the road.

Dan swallowed the grim taste of bile in his throat and looked away as the shot rang through the air, sending parrots squawking into the air from the trees.

"Make yourself useful, City Boy. There's a blue tarp in the back of the ute. Bring it and help me drag her onto it." She threw the command at him without even looking back as she explored the body of the roo. "And while you're there, bring me the little blue sleeping bag. She has a joey."

Shock, anger, regret—the emotions warred inside him as he stood frozen to the spot. How could he have thought a tree change would make a difference? What was he thinking? Even out here in the middle of nowhere he was ruining lives, destroying families. The black pull of anxiety tugged at the far reaches of his mind.

He *could* quit now and go back to his corner office with the view of the Sydney Harbour Bridge and the comfort zone of short office hours and long lunches. But then he'd never know if he *could* cut it in the country or not, and he'd never been one to back down from a challenge.

His gaze dropped to his hands where traces of blood from the doorframe had marked his skin—another death on his conscience, another growing bloodstain on the ground to confront him in his nightmares.

He heard the crunch of Alice's boots on the gravel and felt the whoosh of air as she walked past him to the ute. She returned moments later with a pouch under her arm and a small bottle of water and roll of toilet paper in her hands.

"Here," she said, thrusting the bottle and toilet paper under his nose. "Clean up and get the tarp."

Merciless, he thought. Not that he didn't deserve the ranger's anger. He should have known better, expected something like this to happen. He'd read the sad statistics on road kill. Too late now—there was no going back.

He wiped the blood from his hands with the water and toilet paper, then turned in time to see Alice heading towards him with the blue pouch in her arms. All he saw as she brushed past him was a tiny furry head, all eyes, ears and snout, peering out from the gap in the pouch.

He followed her to the ute, watching as she laid the pouch on the front seat against the backrest and secured it with the seatbelt. She reeked of roo poo and the coppery stench of blood and gunpowder.

His stomach rolled again and he swallowed hard against the rising memory of another time when the smell of death had haunted his senses. Perspiration built on his forehead as he fought to keep the rising bile down.

Alice eyed him wryly. "If you throw up, I'll make you walk the forty kilometres into town," she growled. "You should get there by midnight."

Dan stepped back, took a breath and walked around the back of the ute to grab the tarp. He found himself smiling grimly. Roo poo and all, she was a fresh change from the city girls. He couldn't imagine any of them doing what Alice had.

Sure, she was angry and bad-tempered right now—she had the right to be—but under that khaki shirt, those jeans and boots was a pretty neat package. There was definitely something about her, an earthiness that made her real.

He wiped his palms on the backside of his jeans and pulled the tarp over the side of the ute, slinging it over his shoulder. A shaft of pain speared through his chest. Seatbelt burn for his sins, and no doubt tomorrow his muscles would be screaming from the force of impact.

On the way back to the kangaroo, he cast a sad look at his car. Only two thousand k's on the clock and it was probably a write-off. He'd made a typical city boy error. He should have bought something sturdier, something more suited to the country, like Alice's four-wheel drive.

Alice sat crouched at the kangaroo's side. Silently,

he spread the tarp out on the ground and waited for instruction. It was then he noticed the two white crosses at the foot of the giant eucalypt. *RIP Lochie. RIP Pete.* A shiver ran through him. If he'd swerved to avoid the animal, his name could have been on a cross there too.

"Take the tail, Slick. I'll get the light bit."

He looked down to see Alice peering up at him, her arms under the kangaroo's shoulders, ready to shift it onto the tarp. Casting off his morbid thought, he moved to lift the tail. "You're going to pick up that roo."

"That's what I said."

"That thing must weigh a ton."

"It's a female. She's only about forty kilos. What? You think I can't do it?"

"I never said that."

"Then put your back into it before we become a statistic ourselves. On the count of three," said Alice. "One, two, three!"

They placed the roo onto the tarp, carried it to the ute and laid it out on the tray. Alice leapt up into the back and wrapped the carcass firmly in the tarp, tying it up with rope. Jumping back down, she slapped the tailgate shut and snapped the locks into place. Her phone rang and she whipped it out of the top pocket of her shirt.

"Hey, Fred," she greeted warmly. "Yeah, I'm okay. Sure, of course. I'll tell him. What?" The change in her tone—from warm to freezing in seconds—had Dan's head snapping up. She looked at him with a frown and then looked away again, listening to what her caller had to say. "Just my luck. I'll drop him off at Maureen's. Cheers, mate."

Dan waited as she hung up and opened the driver's door of the ute. She tossed the phone on the seat and unbuckled the bundled joey.

"Here, you'll have to hold the joey on the drive back into town. Fred will be down later to tow in your car." The chill in her tone froze any response he might make. "Get in. I'll give you a lift to your mum's."

Wordlessly, he took the joey and hoisted himself into the passenger seat of the ute. As she slid behind the wheel, he wondered what it was that had swung her mood from angry to freeze-out.

Alice breathed and tried not to take in the scent of expensive male cologne filling the cab, or the less inviting pong of roo poo. The latter she was used to, the former brought back too many painful memories.

When she'd spotted the car and roo on her routine patrol to check for roadkill, she almost hadn't stopped, was tempted to keep driving past that goddamn tree and ring the accident in to triple zero instead. Why? Why had Dan Molyneaux chosen that spot to run into trouble?

It had taken every ounce of strength she had to

pull over at the very same place she'd lost her husband and child. The little white crosses, the scarred base of the tree, even the ditch Dan had ended up in—all of them stark reminders of the crash. If he'd swerved, the tree would have claimed another life, and she couldn't have stopped for that. No way in hell.

Her hands shook on the steering wheel and she gripped it tighter, knuckles white against the black leather. Grandad Charlie would have her head if he found out how rude she'd been to Dan. He'd tell her it wasn't the man's fault and things happen for a reason. A sign, he'd call it, a sign it was time to move on.

She snuck a look at the man beside her. Tall with dark brown hair, he was good looking enough to be a model for *Tractor Weekly*, except he was a city boy. She caught the look that softened his features as he gazed down at the joey cuddled to his chest in big strong arms. She watched his long fingers gently stroke the rough fur of its ears then run down the line on its snout. Her stomach clenched with awareness at the tenderness in his touch. No way would she let herself like him for that show of caring. She wanted to hate the man who'd bought the Riverside Pub.

"What happens to the joey now?" he asked, breaking into her thoughts.

"I get him checked out at the vet." She'd never intended to sell the pub, it had been in her family for as long as the town had existed, but with the rejuvenation of Bindarra Creek town, Charlie had convinced her it was time to let go of the past.

"And then?"

She sighed, annoyed at having to make conversation with him. It should have been easy. Sign the pub over, hand him the key and walk away without ever having to step inside the place again. She hadn't opened the door in eight years and she wasn't about to do so now.

"We find him a carer until he's old enough to feed himself, teach him how to be a kangaroo and then set him free where we found him." Oh God, and that meant going back to the tree again—another damn good reason to dislike the man sitting next to her.

Bindarra Creek was a small town, but not so small that she'd run into him every five minutes. She kept herself busy enough to avoid the town events and social gatherings, so avoiding him should be just as easy. Driving past Riverside every day and seeing the doors open for business again would be like a stake to her heart because as surely as Dan Molyneaux had killed that kangaroo, the Riverside Pub had killed her husband and child.

Out the corner of her eye, she glimpsed Dan running a hand through his GQ-styled hair. Everything about him screamed success. So what was an up-and-coming exec doing in their little backwater town? Suspicion reared its ugly head. Her own reservations aside, with developers flooding into town and scammers taking advantage of it, she held more than a little resentment towards the council's idea of rejuvenation. But as Charlie had so wisely said, it was the only way to stop Bindarra Creek becoming another ghost town on the map. Not that it was much more than that at the moment.

As the town came into view, Dan spoke. "Look, I'm really sorry about the kangaroo. If I could have stopped in time, I would have. I feel really shit. I've never killed so much as a cockroach in my life."

Alice threw him a doubtful look before slowing down to the forty-kilometre per hour speed limit at the entry to Main Street.

He sighed and tried again. "You obviously already know who I am because you're taking me to Mum's, but I'll introduce myself anyway. I'm Dan Molyneaux. I bought the Riverside Pub."

And by God, he sounded so friggin' chuffed with himself—like a kid with a new toy at Christmas. Her grip tightened on the wheel again and she bit back a sharp retort. Anger—irrational and totally uncalled for —rose hot and fast through her blood. If she'd known what an emotional rollercoaster it would be making the decision to sell, she would have dug her feet in deeper and said no. She took a deep breath and let it out slowly. "I know. I'm the one who sold it to you."

"God bless Karma for introducing us so badly," he mocked. "I am pleased to meet you, Alice. I wish it was under better circumstances." He rubbed the sleeping joey's ears. "I'm sorry I didn't recognise your name before."

She ignored him as she turned into the driveway of the veterinary clinic. A touch of guilt trickled through her. He wasn't to know the whole story. No-one had spoken of the tragic events leading to the accident almost eight years ago, nor had anyone murmured a word when she'd shut the doors and boarded up the windows of the two-storey building overlooking the Akuna River. Charlie had silently helped her move from the upstairs accommodation and into the house at the wildlife sanctuary across Gillies Bridge, where the view of the pub was obscured by the trees.

"Yeah, me too," she said, pulling to a stop in front of the clinic. "I'll drop the joey off first." Getting out of the ute, she walked around and opened his door, holding her arms out for the joey.

Dan went to unclip his seatbelt. "I'll come with you. Make sure he's okay."

"This isn't an episode of *Skippy*, Mr Molyneaux. I take him inside, the vet checks him out and keeps him overnight. This is where your responsibility ends. The rest is up to me."

God, she hated sounding so damn angry. Raw pain slashed at her heart. Why did the man responsible for forcing her out of her comfort zone have to be so friggin' nice when all she could be in return was bitchy? Right now, all she wanted was to curl up in the corner and cry as old wounds reopened and bled inside her.

Until today the sale had been nothing more than a piece of paper, but now the new owner was here in the flesh, reality confronted her with the speed of a freight train.

Dan frowned down at her, but handed over the joey in silence. She took it and cradled it close to her chest, tears choking her throat. Turning away so he wouldn't see them fill her eyes, she hurried toward the clinic.

Dan let out a breath as he watched Alice walk away. Wow, he'd been on the receiving end of a woman's anger many a time, but Bindarra Creek's park ranger was the first to make him feel lower than cockroach droppings. Either she really took her job seriously or she disliked newcomers to their half-awake town, or there was something much, much deeper driving her fury.

He felt like he'd gone ten rounds with Danny Greene and come out of the ring reeling from the punches. Had he just made the biggest mistake of his life? He'd committed career suicide by leaving the city to move to a town where so far, the ride had more downs than the Dow Jones during the GFC. What was he thinking? What did he know about kangaroos and country pubs? Jesus, he barely knew how to pour a beer let alone pull one. *Way to go, Molyneaux.*

Alice opened the driver's side door and got in behind the wheel. She pulled on her seatbelt and started the engine. He wanted to ask if everything was okay but he figured he'd be better off keeping his mouth shut. She must have felt his quick glance on her face because she cast him a look offside.

"The joey's fine. No broken bones and he's dealing with the shock well enough to have a drink. Lucky, he's a little older so his chance of survival without his mum is higher," she said quietly.

"Thanks. It helps to know that." Dan sensed that most of the fight had gone out of her, but judging from her pale cheeks and red-rimmed eyes, whatever had got her going still simmered close to the surface.

"Here." She tossed him a sample bottle of antiseptic hand gel. "Use this to clean your hands. You don't want to get sick. Roos carry a number of germs that aren't pleasant when transferred to humans. There's a tub of wipes at your feet to clean away the blood first."

Great, he thought as he leaned forward to do as she instructed.

They drove in silence back onto Main Street and turned onto Mt Ingalls Street, where he knew Mum had bought an old cottage. The small town grapevine must have let her know they were on their way because there she stood, waiting at the gate with a wooden spoon in her hand.

Dan grinned, the dark cloud lifting a little. Baking was what Mum did when she was worried. God bless her, he hoped that spoon had whipped up a batch of scones and wasn't meant for whipping his arse! She'd had to use a few for the latter in his younger days. He'd grown up better for it.

The months away from the city had been good to her. Although her hair was greyer now, there was a sparkle in her eye and colour in her cheeks he hadn't seen in Sydney. It looked like Bindarra Creek's fresh country air had worked its magic on her. God, he hoped there was some of that magic left over for him.

"This is your stop. Fred will drop off your bags when he tows the car in," murmured Alice as she drew to a halt outside the gate and waved to his mum.

"Thanks for the ride."

"No worries."

Not *it's a pleasure, welcome to town,* just *no worries.* Dan wanted to say more, but his tongue had cleaved to the roof of his mouth and his throat choked around what to say. She turned to roll down her window and greet his mum, while he opened the door and got out.

"Alice, honey, Fred called to tell me where you picked Dan up. Are you okay, love?"

"I'm fine, Maureen, thanks for asking. It was bound to happen sooner or later. Driving past is one thing, having to stop is something else, but I can deal with it. I have to. It's my job."

As Dan stepped onto the pavement, he saw the flicker of pain in Alice's green eyes. He pecked a kiss on his mum's cheek and she pulled him in for a hug with her arm around his waist.

"It's good to have you home, Dan," she said, pressing her cheek against his chest as he dropped a casual arm around her shoulders. "Alice, would you like to come in for a cup of tea and a scone? I have some fresh fig jam for them."

Alice's gaze slipped to Dan's face, then flicked away again. "Thanks, but I'll have to pass. I need to get the carcass to the butchery. There might be enough left to render it for the dogs."

Dan squirmed at the thought. Better than leaving it to the meat ants and other scavengers on the side of the road, he guessed.

"Righto then," Maureen said and squeezed Alice's elbow where it lay on the open window. "Thanks for bringing Dan home."

"Sure."

She turned to face the windscreen, her eyes on the road ahead and Dan thought she looked like she wanted to make a quick getaway.

"Yeah thanks, Alice."

She nodded. "I'll drop off the keys to Riverside in the morning. Follow Main Street all the way until just before the bridge. You'll see the pub on the right-hand side." Her voice broke on the last word and she swallowed hard enough that Dan could see her throat work. "See you later."

Dan frowned as she drove away and his mum dropped her arm from his waist. "I feel like I've made a mistake coming here." He let her turn out from under his arm and followed her up the pathway to the house.

"Of course you haven't. What makes you think you have?" She pulled open the painted metal flyscreen and waved him inside.

The cool of the air conditioning chilled his skin as he followed her down the hall, past the lounge room with its faded wallpaper behind her favourite armchair, and into the old kitchen where the smell of freshly baked scones teased his senses.

"The accident, the roo, the pub, Alice—" He shrugged. "Signs all pointing to this being a bad idea."

Maureen sighed heavily. "Sit down, Dan. I'll make you a cup of tea and then I'll fill you in on a few of the skeletons in Bindarra Creek's closet."

BINDARRA CREEK – A TOWN
REBORN

Welcome to Bindarra Creek, a struggling country town
where people work hard and love deeply. Set in the
picturesque tablelands of New England, Australia,
Bindarra Creek is a fictional, drought stricken
community full of intrigue, adventure, drama and
romance.
Life and love in a small country town has never been
more challenging.
Bindarra Creek A Town Reborn series consists of eight
romances written by eight Australian authors and
published individually (beginning in July 2019).

In order of release:
Take Me Home – Suzanne Gilchrist (aka S E
Gilchrist)

In the Heat of the Night – Susanne Bellamy
No Looking Back - Linda Charles
Worth the Wait – Annie Seaton
With Every Breath – Lauren K. McKellar
Stealing Her Heart – Simone Angela
A Twist of Fate – Erin Moira O'Hara
Promise Me Forever – Juanita Kees

To date there are three group writing venture 'series' set in our fictional small town of Bindarra Creek all written by best-selling Australian romance authors. Our latest series is A Town Reborn. A Collection of short romances, Bindarra Creek Short & Sweet, was released in January 2019 and our first series, A Bindarra Creek Romance, was released during 2015/2016.
All books are available as ebooks, some also have paperback versions.
Each series has one theme running throughout, while every romance depicts the changing lives of the townsfolk as our small town begins to grow and thrive despite the dramas of everyday life.

Bindarra Creek Short & Sweet Collection comprised of:
What's in a Kiss – Linda Charles

My Forever Valentine – Sandie James
Pearls and Green Beer – Susanne Bellamy
Full Circle – Annie Seaton
Date with Destiny – Erin Moira O'Hara
A Letter From the Queen – Lee Christine
Love's Sweet Challenge – Suzanne Gilchrist (aka S E Gilchrist)
The Widow Maker – Lauren K. McKellar
Out of the Blue – Noelle Clark

For more info on Bindarra Creek Romances, please visit
www.bindarracreekromance.com

ABOUT THE AUTHOR
Finding love and hope in small country towns with dark secrets ...

Juanita escapes the real world by reading and writing Australian Rural Romance novels with elements of suspense, Australian Fantasy Paranormal and Small Town USA stories. Her romance novels star spirited heroines who give the hero a run for his money before giving in. She creates emotionally engaging worlds steeped in romance, suspense, mystery and intrigue, set in dusty, rural outback Australia and on the NASCAR racetracks of America.

Her small town and Australian rural romances have made the Amazon bestseller and top 100 lists. Juanita writes mostly contemporary and Australian rural romantic suspense but also likes to dabble in the ponds of fantasy and paranormal with Greek gods brought to life in the 21st century.

When she's not writing, Juanita is mother to three boys and has a passion for fast cars and country living.

Author Site: juanitakees.com

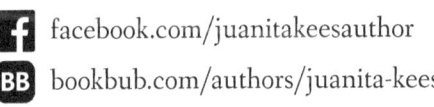

facebook.com/juanitakeesauthor

bookbub.com/authors/juanita-kees

goodreads.com/juanitak

twitter.com/juanitakees